# PIONEERS IN MEDICINE

## FROM THE CLASSICAL WORLD TO TODAY

INVENTORS AND INNOVATORS

# PIONEERS IN MEDICINE

## *FROM THE CLASSICAL WORLD TO TODAY*

EDITED BY SHERMAN HOLLAR

Britannica
Educational Publishing
IN ASSOCIATION WITH
ROSEN
EDUCATIONAL SERVICES

Published in 2013 by Britannica Educational Publishing
(a trademark of Encyclopædia Britannica, Inc.)
in association with Rosen Educational Services, LLC
29 East 21st Street, New York, NY 10010.



Distributed exclusively by Rosen Educational Services.
For a listing of additional Britannica Educational Publishing titles, call toll free (800) 237-9932.

First Edition

Britannica Educational Publishing
J.E. Luebering: Director, Core Reference Group, Encyclopædia Britannica
Adam Augustyn: Assistant Manager, Encyclopædia Britannica

Anthony L. Green: Editor, Compton's by Britannica
Michael Anderson: Senior Editor, Compton's by Britannica
Andrea R. Field: Senior Editor, Compton's by Britannica
Sherman Hollar: Associate Editor, Compton's by Britannica

Marilyn L. Barton: Senior Coordinator, Production Control
Steven Bosco: Director, Editorial Technologies
Lisa S. Braucher: Senior Producer and Data Editor
Yvette Charboneau: Senior Copy Editor
Kathy Nakamura: Manager, Media Acquisition

Rosen Educational Services
Hope Lourie Killcoyne: Executive Editor
Nelson Sá: Art Director
Cindy Reiman: Photography Manager
Karen Huang: Photo Researcher
Brian Garvey: Designer, Cover Design
Introduction by Hope Lourie Killcoyne

**Library of Congress Cataloging-in-Publication Data**

Pioneers in medicine: from the classical world to today/edited by Sherman Hollar.
p. cm.—(Inventors and innovators)
"In association with Britannica Educational Publishing, Rosen Educational Services."
Includes bibliographical references and index.
ISBN 978-1-61530-669-5 (library binding)
1. Medicine—History—Juvenile literature. 2. Medical innovations—History—Juvenile literature. I. Hollar, Sherman.
R133.5.P46 2013
610—dc23

2011040173

*Manufactured in the United States of America*

Cover, p. 3 © www.istockphoto.com/Chepko Danil Vitalevich; interior background image (pipette and petri dish) © www.istockphoto.com/malerapaso

# CONTENTS

# INTRODUCTION

*Edward Jenner makes history—and in this 18th-century depiction, draws a small gathering of onlookers—as he inoculates an eight-year-old boy with cowpox virus, the first such procedure of its kind.* Three Lions/Hulton Archive/Getty Images

One sure way to both help humanity and gain a place in history is to tackle a seemingly unstoppable disease. For Walter Reed it was yellow fever. For Jonas Salk, polio. But in order to create a cure, one must break with the past. And doing things that have not been done before—especially when lives are on the line—can lead to opposition. Take the case of Edward Jenner. As a young apprentice to a doctor in 18th-century England, Jenner had heard a farm girl tell the doctor that she could not contract smallpox because she had already had cowpox. Years later, after much experimenting with that notion of resistance based on prior exposure, Jenner, then a doctor himself, went so far as to inject a healthy eight-year-old boy with cowpox. Two months later he exposed him to smallpox. Jenner's experiment was met with scorn and incredulity. But it worked. And so in time, enough other doctors started using the same preventative method, one which Jenner had given a now-familiar name: vaccination.

Sometimes a medical advance was as basic as insisting upon cleanliness—namely, noticing that the simple act of washing hands could stop the spread of infection. Such was the now elementary but then revolutionary contribution of 19th-century Hungarian physician Ignaz Semmelweis.

That notion of maintaining sanitary conditions was one that 19th-century English nurse Florence Nightingale championed as well. In her case, doing so in the military hospitals of Scutari, Turkey—used as a troop base during war between England and Russia—was extremely challenging. There, soldiers were dying more as a result of infection than of battlefield wounds. By her own rigorous insistence upon sanitary regulations, as well as the introduction of special diets, Nightingale brought down the death rate from 45 to 2 percent. And for the renowned 19th-century German physician Rudolf Virchow, public cleanliness and proper hygiene became something of a crusade, Virchow going so far as to design the sewage system of Germany's capital, Berlin.

If at first you don't succeed, inoculate, inoculate again. Such might be the motto for 19th-century French chemist Louis Pasteur. Best known for his discovery of the pasteurization process, in 1882 Pasteur turned his attention to rabies, beginning careful and repeated trials in which he attempted to halt the development of rabies in infected animals. He eventually succeeded in curing an infected dog after inoculating the animal 14 times.

And it just so happened that three years later, the number 14 would again resurface in regard to rabies for Pasteur, as it happened to be the number of times that a nine-year-old boy had been bitten by a rabid dog. Though reluctant to try his remedy on a human, at the fervent request of the boy's mother, Pasteur did so. The wounds healed and no rabies appeared, making the boy the first human saved by Pasteur's cure.

As readers travel through time in this book meeting healers through the ages, they will also discover tidbits about the lives of those profiled, such as which doctor was challenged to a duel by German chancellor-to-be Otto von Bismarck, which famous doctor married the great-granddaughter of Paul Revere, which nurse was arrested and jailed for her efforts to educate women about birth control, and which psychiatrist came up with the now-ubiquitous personality designations of introvert and extrovert. (Nope, not Freud.)

From Asclepius, the mythic Greek god of medicine, to Hippocrates, the father of medicine, and on to inspiring medical mavericks such as Alexander Fleming, who brought the world penicillin, and Margaret Chan, whose leadership helped avert the widespread outbreak of deadly diseases, *Inventors and Innovators: Pioneers in Medicine: From the Classical World to Today* presents a clear, concise, and captivating compendium of those who have improved the health and welfare of millions the world over.

# CHAPTER 1

# ASCLEPIUS

The Greek god of medicine, Asclepius—in Latin, Aesculapius—was the son of Apollo (god of healing, truth, and prophecy) and the mortal princess Coronis. Asclepius was brought up by the centaur Chiron, who taught him the art of healing. At length Zeus (the king of the gods), afraid that Asclepius might render all men immortal, slew him with a thunderbolt. Apollo slew the Cyclopes (monstrous one-eyed giants) who had made the thunderbolt and was then forced by Zeus to serve Admetus, son of the king of Pherae in Thessaly. The words *panacea*, a nonexistent remedy for illness, and *hygiene*, conditions and practices conducive to health, come from Asclepius's two daughters, Panacea and Hygieia.

Homer, in the *Iliad*, mentions Asclepius only as a skillful physician and the father of two Greek doctors at Troy, Machaon and Podalirius; in later times, however, he was honored as a hero and eventually worshiped as a god. The cult of Asclepius

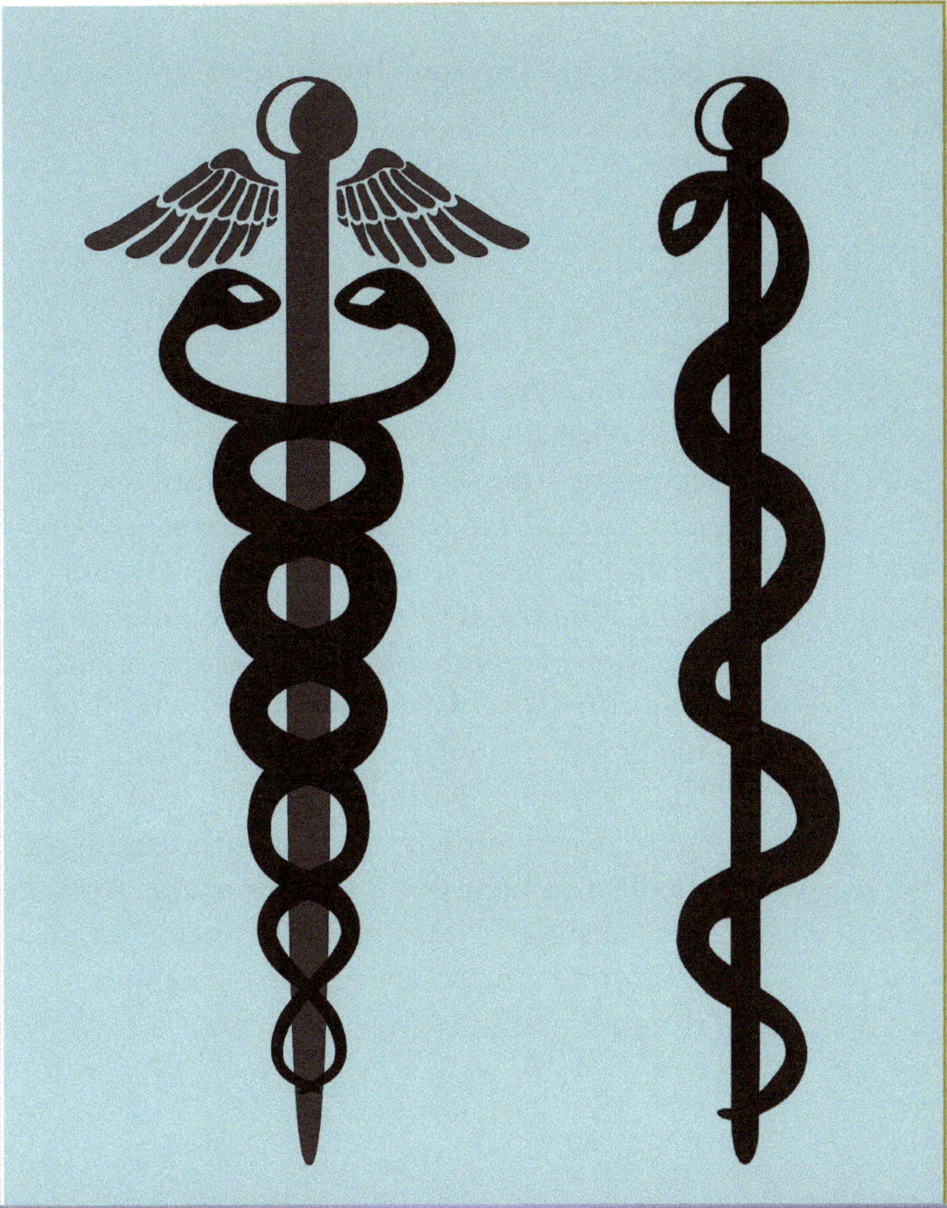

The caduceus, left, is often thought to be the symbol of medicine, but it is the staff on the right that is the true emblem. Shutterstock.com

began in Thessaly but spread to many parts of Greece. Because it was supposed that Asclepius effected cures of the sick in dreams, the practice of sleeping in his temples in Epidaurus in South Greece became common. In 293 BCE his cult spread to Rome, where he was worshiped as Aesculapius.

Asclepius was frequently represented standing, dressed in a long cloak, with bare breast; his usual attribute was a staff with a serpent coiled around it. The serpent, which was sacred to him, symbolized renewal of youth because it casts off its skin. This staff is the only true symbol of medicine. A similar but unrelated emblem, the caduceus, with its winged staff and intertwined serpents, is frequently used as a medical emblem but is without medical relevance since it represents the magic wand of Hermes, or Mercury, the messenger of the gods and the patron of trade.

# CHAPTER 2

# IMHOTEP

Imhotep served as chief minister, sage, and astrologer to the Egyptian king Djoser (reigned 2630–2611 BCE) and was later worshiped as the god of medicine in Egypt and in Greece, where he was identified with the Greek god of medicine, Asclepius. He is considered to have been the architect of the famous step pyramid at the necropolis of Saqqara in Memphis.

Although no contemporary account has been found that refers to Imhotep as a practicing physician, ancient documents illustrating Egyptian society and medicine during the Old Kingdom (*c.* 2575– *c.* 2130 BCE) show that the chief soothsayer of the pharaoh's court also frequently served as the nation's chief physician. Imhotep's reputation as the reigning genius of the time, his position in the court, his training as a scribe, and his becoming known as a medical demigod only 100 years after his death are strong indications that he must have been a physician of considerable skill.

Not until the Persian conquest of Egypt in 525 BCE was Imhotep elevated to the position of a full deity, replacing Nefertem in the great triad of Memphis, shared with his mythological parents Ptah, the creator of the universe, and Sekhmet, the goddess of war and pestilence. Imhotep's cult reached its zenith during Greco-Roman times, when his temples in Memphis and on the island of Philae in the Nile River were often crowded with sufferers who prayed and slept there with the conviction that the god would reveal remedies to them in their dreams. The only Egyptian mortal besides the 18th-dynasty sage and minister Amenhotep to attain the honor of total deification, Imhotep is still held in esteem by physicians who, like the eminent 19th-century British practitioner Sir William Osler, consider him "the first figure of a physician to stand out clearly from the mists of antiquity."

# CHAPTER 3

# HIPPOCRATES

Hippocrates, a physician from the island of Cos in ancient Greece, is known as the "father of medicine." He has long been associated with the Hippocratic Oath, a document he did not write but which sets forth the obligations, ideals, and ethics of physicians. In a modified form the oath is still often required of medical students upon graduation.

Very little is known of the life of Hippocrates. He was a contemporary of the philosopher Socrates in the 5th century BCE and was mentioned by Plato in two of his *Dialogues*. He was, in his lifetime, quite well known as a teacher and physician, and he appears to have traveled widely in Greece and Asia Minor, practicing medicine and teaching. There was presumably a medical school on Cos, in which he taught frequently. Hippocrates probably belonged to a family that had produced well-known physicians for many generations. Aristotle says in his *Politics* that Hippocrates was

*Hippocrates.* Hulton Archive/Getty Images

called "the Great Physician." Hippocrates died at Larissa in Thessaly.

A small body of writings ascribed to Hippocrates has come down to the present. How many he actually wrote will probably never be known. The number of works in ancient times was 70, but only 60 have been preserved. The earliest surviving copy dates from the 10th century CE.

The works differ greatly in their length, in the opinions expressed, and in the types of intended users. Some are for physicians, some for assistants and students, and some for laymen. A few are philosophical. It is generally agreed that the writings made up the medical library at Cos. During the 3rd or 2nd century BCE they were shipped to the great library at Alexandria, Egypt. Among the titles are *Ancient Medicine, Regimen in Acute Diseases*, *Wounds of the Head*, *Aphorisms*, and *Epidemics*.

CHAPTER 4

# PEDANIUS DIOSCORIDES

Around the year 77 CE, Greek physician and pharmacologist Pedanius Dioscorides produced a five-volume treatise on medicines derived from plants, minerals, and animals—among them, milk, honey, cannabis (marijuana), peppermint, mercury, arsenic, calcium, and opium. This treatise, *De materia medica*, was the foremost classical source of modern botanical terminology and the leading pharmacological text for 16 centuries.

Dioscorides' travels as a surgeon with the armies of the Roman emperor Nero provided him an opportunity to study the features, distribution, and medicinal properties of many plants and minerals. Excellent descriptions of nearly 600 plants are contained in *De materia medica*, and the work deals with approximately 1,000 simple drugs.

The medicinal and dietetic value of animal derivatives such as milk and honey is described in the second book, and a

*Illustrated mandrake entry from Dioscorides' treatise* De materia medica. *In ancient times mandrake was believed to have magical powers. Its forked root, seemingly resembling the human form, is depicted in imaginative detail.* Bibliotheque de L'Arsenal, Paris, France/Archives Charmet/The Bridgeman Art Library

synopsis of such chemical drugs as mercury (with directions for its preparation from cinnabar), arsenic (referred to as auripigmentum, the yellow arsenic sulfide), lead acetate, calcium hydrate, and copper oxide is found in the fifth book. He clearly refers to sleeping potions prepared from opium and mandragora (mandrake, pictured above) as surgical anesthetics.

Although the work may be considered little more than a drug collector's manual by modern standards, the original Greek manuscript, which was copied in at least seven other languages, describes most drugs used in medical practice until modern times and served as the primary text of pharmacology until the end of the 15th century. Modern editions have been published in Greek (1906–14) and in English (1934).

# CHAPTER 5

# GALEN

The most significant physician of the ancient world after Hippocrates, Galen achieved great fame throughout the Roman Empire. He was both physician and philosopher and the founder of experimental physiology. His many writings influenced the development of medicine for 1,400 years and were partly responsible for the emergence of science in Europe during the Renaissance.

Galen was born in 129 CE in Pergamum (now Bergama) in Asia Minor. In that city was the chief shrine of Asclepius, the god of healing. Attached to the shrine was a school of medicine, where the young Galen met many of the famous teachers and philosophers of his time. There was also a troupe of gladiators maintained by the school's director. These provided Galen and other students of medicine the chance to study wounds and the effects of medical treatment. Galen continued his studies in Smyrna and for a time wandered about the

Middle East, taking time to visit the great medical school at Alexandria in Egypt. In 157 he returned home and became chief physician to the gladiators.

In 161 Galen traveled to Rome, where he soon earned a reputation as an outstanding healer. About 168 the emperor Marcus Aurelius appointed Galen physician to his son Commodus, who later became emperor. This afforded Galen the opportunity to study and to write. His more than 400 treatises were on many subjects, including philosophy and drama. His many medical writings showed penetrating and often accurate observations on the human anatomy, including heart, liver, kidney, bladder, and nerve functions. Late in the Middle Ages many of his texts were translated by Muslim Arab scholars and eventually found their way into Latin versions. Galen died about 199, probably in Rome.

# Chapter 6

# Avicenna

During the Middle Ages, few scholars contributed more to science and philosophy than the Muslim scholar Avicenna. By his writings he helped convey the thought of the Greek philosopher Aristotle to the thinkers of western Europe, and his *Canon of Medicine* became the definitive work in its field for centuries.

Born in Bukhara, Persia (now in Iran), in 980, he spent his childhood and youth studying Islamic law, literature, and medicine. By age 21 he was considered a great scholar and an outstanding physician.

After his father's death, Avicenna left Bukhara and for about twenty years lived in different Persian cities, working as a physician and completing two of his major works. *The Book of Healing* was a large encyclopedia covering the natural sciences, logic, mathematics, psychology, astronomy, music, and philosophy. It is probably the largest work of its kind ever written by one man. *The Canon of Medicine* was a systematic

*Avicenna, here depicted as the "Persian Galen" by artist Robert A. Thom, 1953.* Courtesy of the National Library of Medicine

exposition of the achievements of Greek and Roman physicians.

For the last 14 years of his life, Avicenna lived in the city of Isfahan and continued his prodigious writing career. He died in 1037.

In the next century much of Avicenna's work was translated into Latin and thereby became available to the philosophers and theologians of Europe. In Islam his contributions in medicine, theology, and philosophy are still recognized as valuable.

# Chapter 7

# Ambroise Paré

Regarded as the father of modern surgery, French physician Ambroise Paré introduced alternatives for many of the painful surgical procedures in use at the time. Out of concern for the suffering of his patients, he avoided surgery whenever possible.

Paré was born in 1510 in Bourg-Hersent, France. While still a young boy he became a barber-surgeon's apprentice at a time when surgery was a specialization within the barbering profession. In about 1529 Paré went to Paris and resumed his apprenticeship at the Hôtel-Dieu hospital. He was taught anatomy and surgery and in 1537 was employed as an army surgeon. By 1552 his expertise was so acclaimed that he was enlisted as surgeon for four successive kings of France: Henry II, Francis II, Charles IX, and Henry III.

Paré entered the army when gunshot wounds were still being treated with boiling oil because they were considered poisonous.

It is said that one night in camp, when the supply of boiling oil ran out, Paré discovered his alternative and less painful wound treatment—a mixture of egg yolk, rose oil, and turpentine. The discovery was a great improvement over the old treatment; however, because Paré's report of his findings was written in French rather than in Latin, it was ridiculed by his more educated but less practically schooled colleagues.

Another of Paré's medical contributions was his reintroduction of the tying off of arteries to control bleeding. This technique replaced the older method of searing vessels with hot irons. Paré was one of the first surgeons to discard the practice of castrating patients who required hernia surgery. He also improved obstetrical methods, invented many scientific instruments, and was the first to suggest that syphilis was a cause of aneurysm, the out-pouching of blood vessels. Paré also introduced the implantation of teeth, artificial limbs, and artificial eyes made of gold and silver. He died on Dec. 20, 1590, in Paris.

CHAPTER 8

# Andreas Vesalius

The science of biology and the practice of medicine were revolutionized by the Flemish physician and surgeon Vesalius in the 16th century. By careful and painstaking dissections of cadavers he learned a great deal about the structure of the human body and laid the foundation for modern physiology.

Vesalius was born in December 1514 in Brussels into a family of physicians and pharmacists. He attended the University of Louvain (1529–33) and spent the next three years at the medical school of the University of Paris. In 1536 he returned home to spend another year at Louvain. He received his doctorate in medicine in 1537 and then worked in Padua as a lecturer in surgery. His anatomical studies led him to break with the theories of the Greek physician Galen, whose writings on physiology had long been considered authoritative. In 1543 Vesalius published his *Seven Books on the Structure of the Human Body*, the most accurate such work on the subject up to that time.

In the same year Vesalius presented a copy of his work to Emperor Charles V, who appointed him court physician. From 1553 to 1556 Vesalius was in Brussels, occupied with a flourishing medical practice. Three

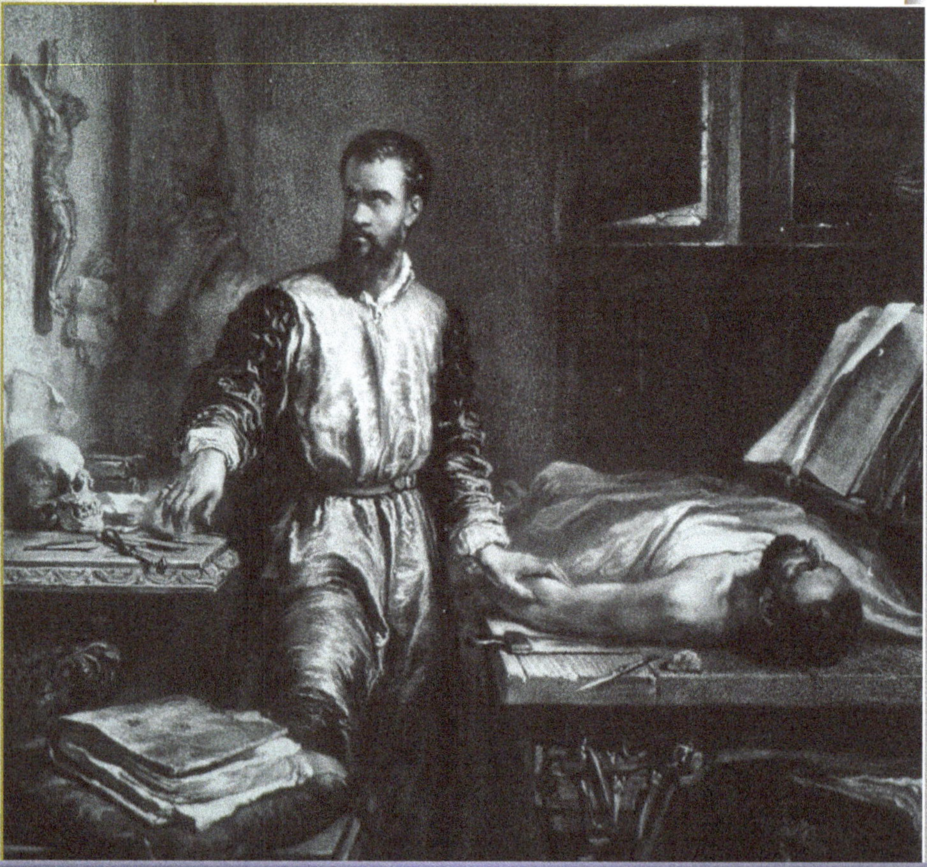

*Andreas Vesalius preparing to dissect a cadaver.* Courtesy of the National Library of Medicine

years later he went to Madrid to take up an appointment as physician to the court of Philip II. He remained in Madrid until 1564, when he was allowed to make a pilgrimage to Jerusalem. On the way back he became ill, and he died on the Greek island of Zacynthus in June 1564.

# CHAPTER 9

# WILLIAM HARVEY

From dissecting many creatures, including humans, English physician William Harvey discovered the nature of blood circulation and the function of the heart as a pump. Before his discoveries blood was thought to ebb and flow through the body by the contraction of arteries. Harvey's work also laid down the foundations of physiology, the study of body functions.

William Harvey was born on April 1, 1578, in Folkestone, Kent, England. He was the oldest of the seven sons of Thomas Harvey. At age 10 he was sent to the King's School in Canterbury, and at 16 he entered Gonville and Caius College, Cambridge, where he received a bachelor's degree in 1597.

Harvey then studied medicine at the University of Padua in Italy, the finest medical school of its time. One of his teachers was Hieronymus Fabricius, a noted surgeon and anatomist who had already discovered the one-way valves in veins, but was not sure of their purpose. Harvey later proved that they prevent blood from flowing backward. He returned to London after receiving his medical degree in 1602.

Shortly after his return to England Harvey married Elizabeth Browne, daughter of a physician to Queen Elizabeth I. In 1607 he received a fellowship at the Royal College of Physicians, and in 1609 he became assistant physician. He was then a physician at St. Bartholomew's Hospital until 1643.

In 1618 Harvey was appointed one of the physicians to King James I. When King Charles I ascended to the throne Harvey became his personal physician. King Charles took a personal interest in Harvey's research in circulation and growth, and he provided Harvey with animals for experimentation.

From 1615 to 1656 Harvey was appointed to a college lectureship. The manuscript of the notes on which the lectures were based is entitled *Lectures on the Whole of Anatomy*. His book *On the Motion of the Heart and Blood in Animals*, published in 1628, gave a unique and accurate account of the circulatory system. The book made Harvey

EXERCITATIO
ANATOMICA DE
MOTV CORDIS ET SAN-
GVINIS IN ANIMALI-
BVS,
GVILIELMI HARVEI ANGLI,
Medici Regii, & Professoris Anatomiæ in Col-
legio Medicorum Londinensi.

FRANCOFVRTI,
Sumptibus GVILIELMI FITZERI.
ANNO M. DC. XXVIII.

*Title page of the first edition of* On the Motion of the Heart and Blood in Animals, *published in 1628, in which Harvey explains blood circulation.* Hulton Archive/ Getty Images

famous throughout Europe despite initial attacks on it.

Harvey explained that blood does not contain bubbles of air. He proved that blood does not pass through the heart's septum, and he explained the function of the valves in the heart and larger veins. Harvey died in London on June 3, 1657.

## Chapter 10

# Marcello Malpighi

The Italian physician and biologist Marcello Malpighi founded the sciences of microscopic anatomy and histology. For more than 40 years he used microscopes of his own making to study and describe animal tissue. Through these lenses he was able to see the specific subdivisions of such organs as the liver, spleen, brain, and kidney. His research provided a foundation for later advances in physiology, embryology, and practical medicine. During his lifetime, however, he was caught in a conflict between ancient and modern medicine. The envy of his colleagues led, in 1684, to the destruction of his home, papers, books, and apparatuses.

Malpighi was born in Crevalcore on March 10, 1628. In 1653 he was granted doctorates in both medicine and philosophy from the University of Bologna. He taught there until 1656, when he was invited to the University of Pisa. He returned to Bologna in 1659, but after three years took a post at the University of Messina in Sicily. By 1667 he was back in Bologna again. Malpighi's work aroused the interest of the Royal Society in London. In 1669 he was named an honorary member, and from then on all his papers were published in London.

After his work was destroyed, he was invited in 1691 to become personal physician to Pope Innocent XII in Rome as recognition for his work. He was named a count and elected to the College of Doctors of Medicine. Malpighi died in Rome on Nov. 30, 1694.

# Chapter 11

# Anthony van Leeuwenhoek

By means of his extraordinary ability to grind lenses, Anthony van Leeuwenhoek greatly improved the microscope as a scientific tool. This led to his doing a vast amount of innovative research on bacteria, protozoa, and other small life-forms that he referred to as "animalcules" (tiny animals) and "wretched beasties."

Leeuwenhoek was born in Delft, Holland, on Oct. 24, 1632. He probably did not have much scientific education, for his family could not afford it. He first became a haberdasher (a dealer in men's clothing and accessories) and draper and, in 1660, chamberlain to the sheriffs at Delft. His hobby was lens grinding; and in his lifetime he ground about 400 lenses, most of which were quite small, with a magnifying power of from 50 to 300 times.

It was not only his lenses that made him world famous but also his work with the microscope. His keen powers of observation led to discoveries of major significance. For example, he observed and calculated the sizes of bacteria and protozoa and gave the first accurate description of red blood cells.

Although Leeuwenhoek lived in Delft, he maintained a regular correspondence with the Royal Society of England, to which he was elected in 1680. Most of his discoveries were published in the society's *Philosophical Transactions*. He continued his work throughout most of his 90 years. He died in Delft on Aug. 26, 1723.

CHAPTER 12

# William Cheselden

William Cheselden, a British surgeon and teacher of anatomy and surgery, wrote *Anatomy of the Human Body* (1713) and *Osteographia, or the Anatomy of the Bones* (1733). The former was used as a text by anatomy students for nearly a century.

Born on Oct. 19, 1688, in Somerby, England, Cheselden was apprenticed as a youth to Mr. Wilkes, a surgeon of Leicester. He also studied under the anatomist William Cowper in 1703 and under James Ferne, a surgeon and lithotomist (specialist in removal of bladder stones) at St. Thomas' Hospital. By 1711 he was already established as a lecturer in anatomy. Cheselden was named assistant surgeon at St. Thomas' in 1718 and was elected one of the institution's principal surgeons the following year. Queen Caroline appointed him to be her surgeon in 1727. In 1733 he published *Osteographia*, an atlas of the bones of the human body that was widely celebrated for the beauty and accuracy of its illustrations.

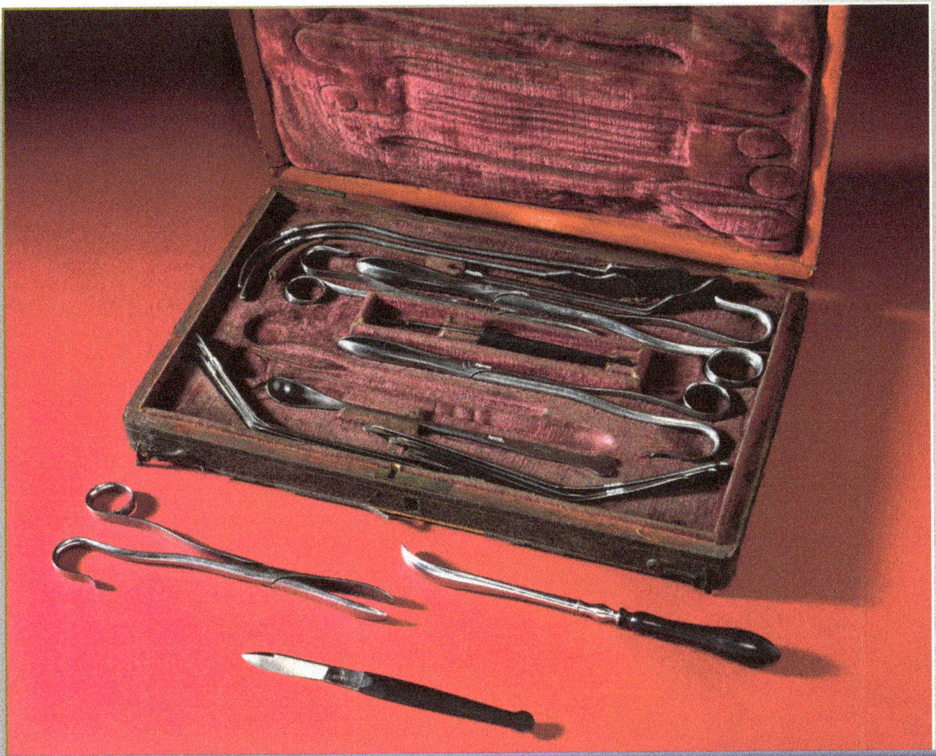

*Late 18th-century tools of the lithotomic trade, such as might have been used by William Cheselden.* SSPL via Getty Images

Cheselden was known for his swift and skillful operations; it was reported that he could perform a lithotomy in 54 seconds. He was, in 1727, the first surgeon to extract bladder stones using the lateral approach (making an incision to one side of the bladder) rather than the suprapubic approach (in which the incision is made above the pubic bone); the lateral technique was soon used by surgeons throughout Europe. The following year Cheselden surgically restored a blind man's vision and devised a method of treatment for some forms of blindness in which an opening, created by surgery, functioned as an "artificial pupil." Cheselden died on April 10, 1752, in Bath.

## CHAPTER 13

# EDWARD JENNER

For centuries smallpox was a scourge. The dread disease killed or left weakness and hideous scars. When late in the 18th century Edward Jenner, a young physician, startled the medical profession by claiming that people who had had cowpox would not get smallpox, his theory was scorned. After many years, however, doctors began using Jenner's method, based upon his theory, of preventing smallpox. He called the method vaccination. By 1979 the disease was declared eradicated.

Edward Jenner was born on May 17, 1749, in Berkeley, Gloucestershire, England, the son of a parish vicar. When he was 13 he decided to be a physician and began as an apprentice to Dr. Daniel Ludlow, who lived near Bristol. One day he heard a young farm girl tell the doctor that she could not contract smallpox because she had once had cowpox. This was the beginning of Jenner's theory and experiments related to it. In 1770 he became the house pupil of the eminent London surgeon and anatomist John Hunter. Hunter was the ideal inspiration for Jenner, with his critical mind, broad interest in biology, disciplined powers of observation, and interest in and skill for scientific experimentation and investigation. The two men formed a lasting friendship, though in 1773 Jenner returned to Berkeley in order to begin his own medical practice.

Jenner continued to experiment with cowpox. He found that there were two forms but that only one provided immunity against smallpox. This one—true cowpox—was a modified form of the more infectious and contagious smallpox. At last he was ready to test his theories. In 1796 Jenner inoculated a healthy eight-year-old boy, James Phipps, with cowpox. Two months later he exposed the child to smallpox, but the boy did not get the disease. Jenner wrote a paper in 1798 explaining his experiments, but it was received coldly in medical circles. He then went to London to demonstrate his theory. No one would submit to vaccination. Discouraged, Jenner returned to Berkeley. Meanwhile, a successful vaccination by a London physician revived interest in Jenner's theory. The medical world was finally convinced.

Many honors came to Jenner. The British government granted him large sums of money to carry on his work. Jenner died in Berkeley on Jan. 26, 1823.

# Chapter 14

# Ignaz Semmelweis

One of the pioneers of modern medicine was a Hungarian physician, Ignaz Semmelweis. With dramatic simplicity he showed how puerperal fever (often called childbed fever) could be virtually wiped out. In Semmelweis's time this disease killed a large percentage of patients in maternity clinics.

Ignaz Philipp Semmelweis was born in Buda (now part of Budapest, with Pest), Hungary, on July 1, 1818. He received his Doctor of Medicine degree from the University of Vienna in 1844. Soon afterward he became an assistant at the maternity clinic of Vienna General Hospital.

While studying the records at this hospital Semmelweis noticed that the death toll from puerperal fever was considerably lower in the section of the clinic staffed by midwives (women trained in obstetrical care) than in the section staffed by doctors and medical students. He knew that the doctors and students often came into the maternity wards directly from the dissecting rooms. Perhaps, Semmelweis reasoned, they carried puerperal infection from dissected bodies to patients in the maternity wards.

To halt this transfer of infection Semmelweis ordered all doctors and students to wash their hands in a chlorine solution before entering the maternity wards. Within a few months deaths from puerperal fever declined dramatically in these wards. Later Semmelweis achieved equally impressive results at the Pest maternity clinic. He died in Vienna on Aug. 13, 1865.

# Chapter 15

# Florence Nightingale

In 1854 the English nurse Florence Nightingale took a small band of volunteers to Turkey to care for soldiers wounded in the Crimean War. There she coped with conditions of crowding, poor sanitation, and shortage of basic supplies. After the war she established nursing as a profession and devoted the rest of her life to improving hospital care.

Florence Nightingale was born on May 12, 1820, to well-to-do parents at their temporary residence in Florence, Italy. Named for her birthplace, she grew up in Derbyshire, Hampshire, and London, where her family maintained temporary homes. Nightingale was educated largely by her father. After her parents refused her request to study nursing at a hospital, Nightingale was persuaded to study parliamentary reports. In three years she was an expert on public health and hospitals.

Over her parents' objections she visited hospitals in England and continental

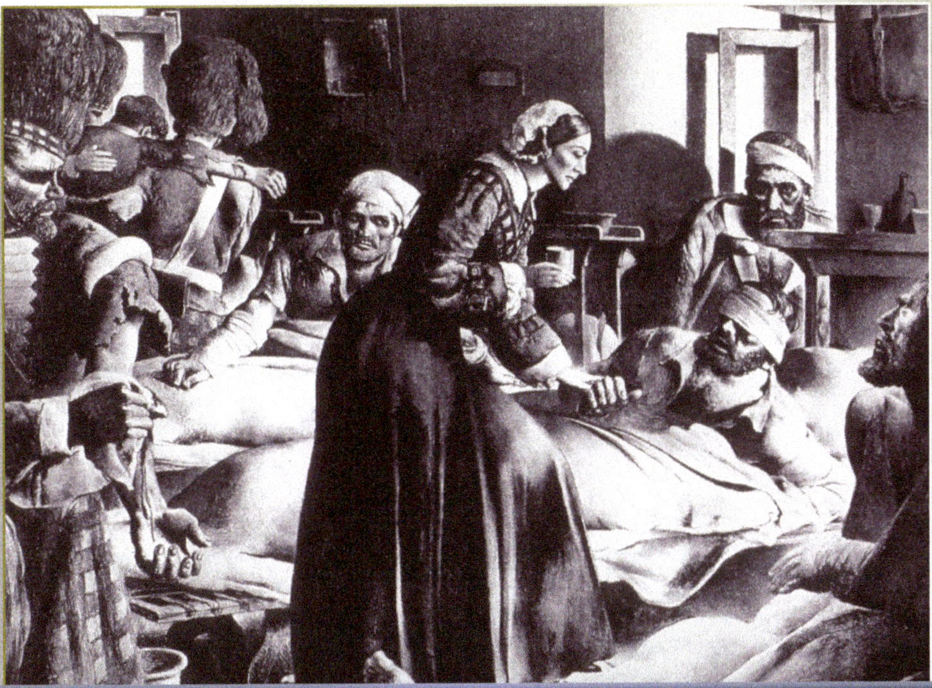

*A lithograph of Florence Nightingale ministering to soldiers in Scutari, Turkey, as depicted by 20th-century American artist Robert Riggs.* Courtesy of the National Library of Medicine

Europe. In 1846 a friend sent her the Year Book of the Institution of Protestant Deaconesses at Kaiserswerth, Germany. Four years later Nightingale entered that same institution and was trained as a nurse. In 1853 she was appointed superintendent of the Institution for the Care of Sick Gentlewomen, in London.

When war with Russia broke out, Nightingale volunteered her services. She was appointed head of the nurses in the military hospitals in Scutari, Turkey. When she arrived more men were dying from fever and infection than from battle wounds. One of Nightingale's first requests was for scrubbing brushes. She enforced sanitary regulations, introduced special diets, and reduced the death rate from 45 to 2 percent. With her own money she bought linen, shirts, food, and even beds for the hospitals. Her health broke. She contracted Crimean fever and nearly died. But she refused to return to England.

By 1856 Florence Nightingale was world famous. She returned to England and met with Queen Victoria and other dignitaries to persuade them to improve conditions for the British soldier. From 1857 she lived as an invalid.

England gave her 50,000 pounds in 1860, which she used to establish the Nightingale School for Nurses. She campaigned by letter for hospital reforms, enforced high professional standards in caring for the sick, and established nursing as a respectable career for women. Nightingale died on Aug. 13, 1910, in London.

# Chapter 16

# Rudolf Virchow

One of the most prominent physicians of the 19th century, German scientist and statesman Rudolf Virchow pioneered the modern concept of the pathological processes of disease. He emphasized that diseases arose, not in organs or tissues in general, but primarily in individual cells. Virchow also contributed to the development of anthropology as a modern science.

Rudolf Carl Virchow was born on Oct. 13, 1821, in Schivelbein, Prussia. He studied at the University of Berlin and graduated as a doctor of medicine in 1843. As a young intern, Virchow published a paper on one of the two earliest reported cases of leukemia; this paper became a classic. In 1849, Virchow was appointed to the chair of pathological anatomy at the University of Würzburg—the first chair of that subject in Germany. In 1856 Virchow became director of the Pathological Institute at the University of Berlin.

Virchow's concept of cellular pathology replaced the existing theory that disease

*Rudolf Virchow.* Courtesy of the National Library of Medicine

arose from an imbalance of the four fluid humors of the body (blood, phlegm, yellow bile, and black bile). He applied the cell theory to disease processes and stated that diseased cells arose from preexisting diseased cells. In 1859 Virchow was elected to the Berlin City Council on which he dealt mainly with such public health matters as sewage disposal, the design of hospitals, meat inspection, and school hygiene. He also designed the new Berlin sewer system. Virchow was elected to the Prussian National Assembly in 1861 and to the German Reichstag in 1880.

Virchow's work in pathological anatomy had led him to begin anthropological work with studies of skulls. He was the organizer of German anthropology, and in 1869 he founded the Berlin Society for Anthropology, Ethnology, and Prehistory. Virchow died on Sept. 5, 1902, in Berlin, Germany.

# Chapter 17

# Elizabeth Blackwell

When Elizabeth Blackwell was graduated as a doctor of medicine in 1849, she became the first woman doctor in the United States. Her enrollment in the Medical Register of the United Kingdom in 1859 made her Europe's first modern woman doctor.

Blackwell was born on Feb. 3, 1821, in Bristol, England. She was one of nine children of Samuel Blackwell, a prosperous sugar refiner. The Blackwells immigrated to New York City in 1832. There the family was active in the abolitionist movement. Their refinery unfortunately did not prosper, and in 1838 they moved to Cincinnati, Ohio. Samuel Blackwell died a few months after the move. The need for the boys to find work and the girls to start school did not prevent the Blackwells from aiding escaped slaves or from participating in intellectual movements.

It was in 1844 that Blackwell determined to become a doctor. Because no medical

*Women medical students studying cadavers at the New York Infirmary for Women and Children. Wood engraving from* Frank Leslie's Illustrated Newspaper, *April 1870.* © Everett Collection/SuperStock

school would admit her, she studied privately with doctors in the South and in Philadelphia. In 1847 the Geneva Medical School of western New York accepted her. The acceptance evoked a storm of ridicule and criticism, but in spite of slights and embarrassments Blackwell pursued her studies. In 1849 she was graduated at the head of her class.

Paris then was the foremost medical center. Blackwell journeyed there to undertake advanced studies, but Paris doctors proved as intolerant as their American colleagues. They would not permit her to study as a doctor. She was forced to enter a large maternity hospital as a student midwife. There she contracted an infection that caused her to lose her sight in one eye. After convalescence, she went to London, where she was permitted to continue her studies.

On her return to New York City in 1850, Blackwell was not permitted to practice in any hospital. She fought for her own and other women's rights to learn and practice. Blackwell started the New York Infirmary for Women and Children, aided by her sister Emily and other women who became doctors and by several tolerant Quakers. Her leadership in meeting the medical problems presented by the Civil War won her recognition. With her sister she opened a medical college for women in her hospital.

Blackwell wrote and lectured. A series of lectures which she delivered in England in 1859 brought her recognition in Britain. After the Civil War she settled in England. Her work and her friendship with Florence Nightingale and other intellectual leaders of the day opened the way for English women to enter the field of medicine.

Her lectures and books dealt largely with social hygiene and with preventive medicine. She died May 31, 1910, at her home in Hastings, England.

# Chapter 18

# Louis Pasteur

The French chemist Louis Pasteur devoted his life to solving practical problems of industry, agriculture, and medicine. Among his discoveries are the pasteurization process and ways of preventing silkworm diseases, anthrax, chicken cholera, and rabies.

Pasteur was born on Dec. 27, 1822, in Dôle, France. In 1827 his family moved to nearby Arbois, where Louis went to school. When he was 17 he received a degree of bachelor of letters at the Collège Royal de Besançon. In 1847, after completing his studies at the École Normale Supérieure, he was appointed professor of chemistry at the University of Strasbourg. Here he met Marie Laurent, daughter of the rector of the university. They were married in 1849. Pasteur's wife shared his love for science. They had five children; three died in childhood.

In 1854 Pasteur became professor of chemistry and dean of the school of science at the University of Lille. A local distiller came to him for help in controlling the process of making alcohol by fermenting beet sugar. Pasteur saw that fermentation was not a simple chemical reaction but took place only in the presence of living organisms. He learned that fermentation, putrefaction, infection, and souring are caused by germs, or microbes.

Pasteur published his first paper on the formation of lactic acid and its function in souring milk in 1857. Further studies developed the valuable technique of pasteurization, a heat-treatment process that destroys pathogenic (disease-causing) microbes in certain foods and beverages. The same year he was appointed manager and director of scientific studies at his old school, the École Normale Supérieure. During the next several years he extended his studies into the germ theory. He spent much time proving to doubting scientists that germs do not originate spontaneously in matter but enter from the outside.

In 1865 Pasteur was asked to help the French silk industry, which was near ruin as a result of a mysterious disease that attacked the silkworms. After intensive research, he discovered that two diseases were involved, both caused by bacteria on the mulberry leaves that provided food for the worms. The diseases were transmitted through the eggs to the next generation of worms. Pasteur showed the silkworm breeders how to identify healthy eggs under the microscope, how to destroy diseased eggs and worms, and how to prevent formation of disease bacteria on the mulberry leaves.

At 45 Pasteur was struck by paralysis. For a time recovery was uncertain, and he was confined to bed for months. The attack left its mark; for the rest of his life, one foot dragged a little as he walked.

In 1877 Pasteur began to seek a cure for anthrax, a disease that killed cattle, sheep, and other farm animals. He drew on research he was conducting on another animal disease, chicken cholera. When he inoculated healthy chickens with weakened cultures of the cholera microbes, the chickens suffered only a mild sickness and were thereafter immune to the disease. Pasteur successfully applied this technique of immunization to the prevention of anthrax.

Pasteur next turned his attention to researching rabies, a disease that slowly

*Louis Pasteur, pictured with a group of English children. Bitten by rabid dogs, the children were sent to him for treatment.* Popperfoto/Getty Images

destroys the central nervous system by attacking the spinal cord. Human beings contract rabies when they are bitten by a dog or another animal that is suffering from the disease. Pasteur reasoned that it might be possible to immunize people after they had been bitten but before destruction of the spinal cord began. He took spinal cord tissues of animals that had died of rabies and dried them for varying periods of time. He then made inoculations of the tissues and injected them into stricken animals. After repeated failures, he finally succeeded in halting the development of rabies in an infected dog. The treatment required 14 inoculations.

Pasteur hesitated to try the remedy on humans, however. The decision was forced on him in 1885 when the mother of a nine-year-old boy begged Pasteur to save her son. The boy had been bitten 14 times by a rabid dog. Pasteur treated the child. The wounds healed and no trace of rabies appeared.

An international fund-raising campaign was subsequently launched to establish a great research laboratory, the Pasteur Institute in Paris, the inauguration of which took place on Nov. 14, 1888. Pasteur died near Saint-Cloud, France, on Sept. 28, 1895.

# Chapter 19

# Henri Dunant

Swiss humanitarian and author Henri Dunant founded the Red Cross (now the Red Cross and Red Crescent), an international agency that aids in the prevention and relief of human suffering. He was a cowinner—with French economist Frédéric Passy—of the first Nobel Prize for Peace in 1901.

Jean-Henri Dunant was born on May 8, 1828, in Geneva, Switzerland. In 1859, while on business in northern Italy, he happened to witness the battle of Solferino between the Austrian army and French and Italian forces and helped organize emergency aid services for the many thousands wounded in the battle. Dunant never forgot this experience. In a book he published in 1862, *Un Souvenir de Solférino*, he proposed forming voluntary relief societies around the world to help prevent and alleviate suffering in war and peacetime. He also proposed an international agreement specifying the treatment of those wounded in war. In

*Henri Dunant in 1902.* © Photos.com/Jupiterimages

1864, the year he founded the Red Cross, the first Geneva Convention came into being. The Geneva Convention provided for (1) the immunity from capture and destruction of all establishments for the treatment of wounded and sick soldiers and their personnel, (2) the impartial reception and treatment of all combatants, (3) the protection of civilians providing aid to the wounded, and (4) the recognition of the Red Cross symbol as a means of identifying persons and equipment covered by the agreement.

Having gone bankrupt because he neglected his business affairs, Dunant left Geneva in 1867. Although he spent most of the rest of his life in poverty, he continued to promote interest in the treatment of prisoners of war, the abolition of slavery, international arbitration, disarmament, and the establishment of a Jewish homeland. He died on Oct. 30, 1910, in Heiden, Switzerland.

# CHAPTER 20

# ROBERT KOCH

A German country doctor, Robert Koch helped raise the study of microbes to the modern science of bacteriology. By painstaking laboratory research, Koch at last demonstrated how specific microbes cause specific diseases.

Robert Heinrich Hermann Koch was born on Dec. 11, 1843, in Clausthal, Germany, a mining town in the Harz Mountains. He made collections of minerals, plants, and small animals and dreamed of being a great explorer. In 1862 he entered the University of Göttingen and began to study medicine. He hoped to serve as an expedition doctor. After graduation, Koch interned at a hospital in Hamburg. In Hamburg he met and married Emmy Fraatz and became a country doctor.

Koch began studying bits of matter through a magnifying glass. He received a microscope from his wife for his 28th birthday and then began his study of anthrax, a deadly disease of warm-blooded animals.

He identified and raised several different cultures.

With these cultures he infected healthy animals in order to demonstrate which microbes produced each type of infection. When he brought the results of his work before scientists at the University of Breslau, in Poland, he demonstrated to the world the first definite proof that a particular microbe causes a particular disease.

In 1882 Koch isolated the tubercle bacillus, the bacterium that causes tuberculosis. The next year he became head of a commission to study cholera in Egypt and India. He announced the discovery of the cholera microbe in 1883. Germany acclaimed him. He was given 25,000 dollars and made director of a great institute to pursue his researches. In 1890 he announced the discovery of tuberculin. This substance, at first wrongly thought to be a cure for tuberculosis, is now widely used to detect the presence of the disease. Koch went on to study tropical diseases in East and West Africa. In 1905 he was awarded the Nobel Prize in Medicine. Koch died on May 28, 1910, in Baden-Baden, Germany.

# Chapter 21

# Alphonse Laveran

French physician, pathologist, and parasitologist Alphonse Laveran discovered the parasite that causes human malaria. For this and later work on protozoal diseases he received the Nobel Prize for Physiology or Medicine in 1907.

Laveran was born on June 18, 1845, in Paris. Educated at the Strasbourg faculty of medicine, he served as an army surgeon in the Franco-German War (1870–71) and practiced and taught military medicine until 1897, when he joined the Pasteur Institute, Paris. While serving as a military surgeon in Algeria in 1880, Laveran discovered the cause of malaria in the course of the autopsies he conducted on malaria victims. He found the causative organism to be a protozoan which he named *Oscillaria malariae*, though it was later renamed *Plasmodium*.

Laveran was a powerful influence in developing research in tropical medicine, carrying on fruitful work in trypanosomiasis, leishmaniasis, and other protozoal diseases, as well as his landmark work in malaria. He established the Laboratory of Tropical Diseases at the Pasteur Institute (1907) and founded the Société de Pathologie Exotique (1908).

Laveran's extensive writings include *Trypanosomes et trypanosomiasis* (with Félix Mesnil; 1904); *Traité des fièvres palustres avec la description des microbes du paludisme* (1884); and *Traité des maladies et épidémies des armées* (1875). Laveran died on May 18, 1922, in Paris.

# Chapter 22

# William Osler

The Canadian physician William Osler won fame as a teacher, clinician, and innovator in his own country as well as in the United States and England. He helped to establish modern teaching methods for medical schools, emphasizing the importance of clinical experience. He is often called the father of internal medicine.

Osler was born in Bond Head, Ont., on July 12, 1849. He was one of nine children of an Anglican minister, the Rev. Featherstone Lake Osler, and Ellen Pickton Osler. A mischievous boy, he was once caned for moving the schoolroom furniture to the attic. Like his father, Osler was expected to be a minister. He became interested in natural history after reading *Religio Medici*, a journal about the mysteries of God, nature, and humanity.

In 1868 he went to Trinity College in Toronto, Ont., but decided that the church was not for him and entered the Toronto Medical School. He then transferred to

*William Osler, c. 1890.* Archive Photos/Getty Images

McGill University's medical school in Montreal, Que., and graduated in 1872.

Osler referred to the activity of the next two years as "brain dusting," traveling and studying in clinics in Great Britain, France, Germany, and Austria. In 1873 he demonstrated that hitherto unidentified bodies in the blood were in fact the third kind of blood corpuscles, which were later named the blood platelets. These corpuscles had been observed before, but no one before Osler had studied them so thoroughly. He returned to Canada and in 1875 became professor of medicine at McGill University. As a pathologist at the Montreal General Hospital, Osler was able to continue his research.

In 1884 he became clinical professor at the University of Pennsylvania. In 1888 he went to the Johns Hopkins Hospital in Baltimore, Md., and later became the first professor of medicine at Johns Hopkins University Medical School. By organizing and transforming the curriculum of clinical teaching, Osler and others made Johns Hopkins a world-famous and respected medical school.

Osler was a professor of medicine at Oxford University from 1905 to 1919. In line with his interests in literature and history, he became a curator of Oxford's Bodleian Library. He wrote and lectured a great deal. His highly influential textbook *The Principles and Practice of Medicine,* published in 1892, inspired John D. Rockefeller to establish the Rockefeller Institute of Medical Research in New York City. In 1892 Osler married Grace Revere Gross, the widow of a colleague and great-granddaughter of Paul Revere. They had two children.

At the coronation of George V, in 1911, Osler was made a baronet. Ill and grief stricken over the loss of his son during World War I, he died in Oxford on Dec. 29, 1919.

# CHAPTER 23

# WALTER REED

One of the leaders in conquering the dreaded disease yellow fever was Walter Reed. Until his time yellow fever ravaged tropical and coastal cities, killing thousands of people in yearly epidemics. As head of the United States Army Yellow Fever Commission, Reed led dramatic experiments to learn how the disease is transmitted. By proving that mosquitoes carry yellow fever, Reed and his coworkers opened the way for control of the disease in all communities where precautions are observed.

Reed was born on Sept. 13, 1851, in Belroi, Va. His father, a Methodist minister, gave him good training in classical subjects and mathematics even during the tumultuous years of the American Civil War. When Walter was 15 his family moved to Charlottesville, Va. A precocious student, he entered the University of Virginia the following year. Although he initially studied classics at the university, he eventually switched to the medical program, completed his medical studies in nine months, and in the summer of 1869, at the age of 18, was graduated as a doctor of medicine. To obtain further clinical experience he matriculated as a medical student at Bellevue Medical College, New York, and a year later took a second medical degree there. After internship he worked for the New York City and Brooklyn boards of health. In 1875 he entered the Army Medical Corps as a first lieutenant. A year of duty in New York was followed by 11 years at various army posts in the West. In 1876 he married Emilie Lawrence; they had two children.

Reed developed a keen interest in the new science of bacteriology. In 1890 he was transferred to duty in Baltimore, Md., and permitted to study at Johns Hopkins Hospital. After three years he was appointed professor of bacteriology and clinical microscopy at the Army Medical School in Washington, D.C.

At the outbreak of the Spanish-American War, Reed headed a committee to investigate epidemics of typhoid fever raging through army camps. The committee found that flies and dust were helping to spread the disease. Reed recommended sanitation measures that reduced the disease rate. His work led to his appointment in 1900 as head of the Yellow Fever Commission, organized to combat the disease among troops stationed in Havana, Cuba.

Reed realized that the pressing need was to find out how yellow fever was being spread. He and his colleagues investigated the theory suggested by earlier researchers that it was mosquitoes rather than contact with fever victims or their clothing or bedding that transmitted the disease. In a series of controlled experiments they proved the theory. At once strict mosquito-control measures were enforced, and yellow fever epidemics ceased.

In 1901 Reed returned to Washington and received many awards. A neglected chronic appendicitis caused his death less than two years later on Nov. 22, 1902. A major medical center in Washington, D.C., is named for him.

# CHAPTER 24

# SANTIAGO RAMÓN Y CAJAL

Spanish histologist Santiago Ramón y Cajal received, with Camillo Golgi, the 1906 Nobel Prize for Physiology or Medicine for establishing the neuron, or nerve cell, as the basic unit of nervous structure. This finding was instrumental in the recognition of the neuron's fundamental role in nervous function and in gaining a modern understanding of the nerve impulse.

Ramón y Cajal was born on May 1, 1852, in Petilla de Aragón, Spain. He obtained a medical degree at the University of Zaragoza in 1873 and became an assistant in the medical faculty there two years later. He served as professor of descriptive anatomy at the University of Valencia (1884–87) and professor of histology and pathological anatomy at the universities of Barcelona (1887–92) and Madrid (1892–1922). He improved Golgi's silver nitrate stain (1903) and developed a gold stain (1913) for the general study of the fine structure of nervous tissue in the brain, sensory centers, and the spinal cords of embryos and young animals. These nerve-specific stains enabled Ramón y Cajal to differentiate neurons from other cells and to trace the structure and connections of nerve cells in gray matter and the spinal cord. The stains have also been of great value in the diagnosis of brain tumors.

In 1920 King Alfonso XIII of Spain commissioned the construction of the Cajal Institute in Madrid, where Ramón y Cajal worked until his death. Among his many books concerning nervous structure is *Estudios sobre la degeneración y regeneración del sistema nervioso,* 2 vol. (1913–14; *The Degeneration and Regeneration of the Nervous System*). Ramón y Cajal died on Oct. 17, 1934, in Madrid.

CHAPTER 25

# KITASATO SHIBASABURO

Japanese physician and bacteriologist Kitasato Shibasaburo helped discover a method to prevent tetanus and diphtheria and, in the same year as French bacteriologist Alexandre Yersin, discovered the infectious agent responsible for the bubonic plague.

Kitasato was born on Jan. 29, 1853, in Kitanosato, Higo province (now Kumamoto prefecture), Japan. He began his study of medicine at Igakusho Hospital (now Kumamoto Medical School). When his mentor, Dutch physician C.G. van Mansvelt, left the school, Kitasato entered Tokyo Medical School (now the Faculty of Medicine, University of Tokyo). After earning his M.D. in 1883, he carried out bacteriological research at the Central Sanitary Bureau of the Ministry of Home Affairs.

In 1885 Kitasato moved to Berlin to join the laboratory of German bacteriologist

*Kitasato Shibasaburo, c. 1911.* Courtesy of the National Library of Medicine

Robert Koch. There, with Emil von Behring, he studied tetanus and diphtheria, two bacterial infections that cause symptoms through the secretion of toxins (a living organism's poisonous waste products). In 1889 Kitasato succeeded in obtaining the first pure culture of the tetanus bacteria (bacilli), and the following year he and von Behring demonstrated that immunity to tetanus could be achieved by injecting a susceptible animal with serum containing antitoxin produced in the blood of an animal exposed to the bacterial toxin. They soon successfully applied this approach, called serum therapy, to the treatment of diphtheria.

Returning to Japan in 1892, Kitasato founded and became president of the Institute for Infectious Diseases, a laboratory near Tokyo that was incorporated in 1899 into the Ministry of Home Affairs. The next year he founded Yojoen, a sanatorium for victims of tuberculosis, and concurrently served as president of both organizations.

Kitasato was sent to Hong Kong in 1894 to investigate an outbreak of the bubonic plague. Within a month he identified the causative organism of the plague, the bacillus *Pasteurella pestis* (now called *Yersinia pestis*; renamed after Alexandre Yersin, who independently discovered the plague bacillus during the Hong Kong epidemic).

In 1914 Kitasato resigned the directorship of the imperial institute and founded the Kitasato Institute. He became the first dean of the medical school of Keio University, an institution he helped establish, in 1917 and held this position until 1928. When the Japanese Medical Association was founded in 1923, he became its first president. In 1924 the emperor invested him with the title of baron. Kitasato died on June 13, 1931, in Tokyo.

# CHAPTER 26

# PAUL EHRLICH

"We must learn to shoot microbes with magic bullets," Paul Ehrlich often exclaimed. By "magic bullets" Ehrlich meant chemicals that would kill disease microbes in the body. His most spectacular discovery was the "magic bullet" Salvarsan, which was long used to treat syphilis. Equally important was his "side chain" theory, dealing with the way the body fights off certain disease poisons. Ehrlich also discovered a way to standardize the manufacture of antidiphtheria serum, and he made important contributions to the knowledge of cancer. In 1908 Ehrlich was the cowinner of the Nobel Prize for Medicine.

Ehrlich, the son of Jewish innkeepers, was born in Silesia (now a part of Poland) on March 14, 1854. He received his M.D. degree from the University of Leipzig in 1878. He served as assistant to Robert Koch. In 1896 he became director of the Institute for Serum Study near Berlin, Germany.

One of Ehrlich's first discoveries was a dye that would move through the body and

*Paul Ehrlich.* National Library of Medicine, Bethesda, Maryland

deposit only at nerve endings. In 1907 he compounded a dye he called trypan red. When injected into mice it destroyed the microbes called trypanosomes.

Trypanosomes are similar to the *Treponema pallidum*, the microbe that causes syphilis, a disease that is most often—though not always —transmitted by sexual contact. In 1909, after 605 failures, Ehrlich and his assistants found an arsenic compound that acted against syphilis as trypan red did against trypanosomes. They named the compound Salvarsan. The following year Ehrlich announced his "side chain" theory of immunity.

Ehrlich was nervous and energetic but cool and precise when he worked. He often said, "It is because we are not exact that we fail." Ehrlich died at Bad Homburg, Germany, on Aug. 20, 1915.

# Chapter 27

# Sigmund Freud

The noted Viennese physician Sigmund Freud was one of the first to suggest workable cures for mental disorders. Although Freud's theories were at first disputed, his work became the foundation for treating psychiatric disorders by psychoanalysis. In more recent times his theories have once again been challenged.

Sigmund Freud was born on May 6, 1856, in Freiberg, Moravia (now Píbor, Czech Republic), the son of a wool merchant. His family moved to Vienna, Austria, when he was 4, and he lived there in the same house for the next 78 years.

A youthful interest in science and human personality led him to enter the University of Vienna medical school in 1873. He took his degree in medicine in 1881. After serving as intern and resident physician in a hospital, he further studied the nervous system. In 1885 he was awarded a fellowship for a year's study in Paris. There he worked under Jean-Martin Charcot, a leading authority on hysteria.

*Sigmund Freud c. 1923 with his grandsons Heinz and Ernst. Their mother, Sophie, Freud's daughter, had died in 1920 of complications from Spanish flu.* Imagno/Hulton Archive/Getty Images

He returned to Vienna in 1886 and began medical practice, specializing in nervous diseases. The case histories of Freud's patients provided material for brilliant investigations. He began to be convinced that sexual causes played a major role in many forms of neurosis. He developed the theory known as the Oedipus complex, which focuses on emotional and sexual complications between parents and children. This was fully described in one of his major works, *The Interpretation of Dreams,* published in 1900.

In 1902 Freud invited four colleagues, including his later rival Alfred Adler, to form what became known as the Vienna Psycho-Analytical Society. It grew to include many notable people, including Carl Jung, but by 1911 differences had become bitter, and the group began to break apart.

Freud was Jewish, and when the Nazis invaded Austria in 1938, they burned his books and banned his theories. Friends got him out of Austria to England. He died of cancer of the jaw and palate in London on Sept. 23, 1939.

# Chapter 28

# Carl Jung

Early in his career the Swiss psychologist and psychiatrist Carl Jung was a friend and follower of Sigmund Freud, the founder of psychoanalysis. Jung, however, came to disagree with Freud and established an alternative school, which he called analytical psychology. Aside from Freud, probably no person had a greater influence on modern psychology and psychiatry than did Jung.

Carl Gustav Jung was born in Kesswil, Switzerland, on July 26, 1875. Jung studied medicine at the University of Basel and psychology in Paris. He was a physician in the psychiatric clinic at the University of Zürich from 1900 to 1909 and a lecturer in psychiatry from 1905 to 1913.

Jung met Freud in 1907 and became a devotee of his psychoanalytical theories and a member of a psychoanalytical society dominated by Freud and his followers. Over time, though, Jung came to reject Freud's idea that sexual experiences during infancy

*Carl Jung, c. 1960.* Paul Popper/Popperfoto/Getty Images

are the principal cause of neurotic behavior in adults. Moreover, Jung believed that Freud overemphasized the role of sexual drive. Jung developed an alternative theory of the libido, arguing that the will to live was stronger than the sexual drive. Jung also emphasized analysis of current problems rather than childhood conflicts in the treatment of adults.

In 1912 Jung resigned from the society and founded his own school of psychology in Zürich. His classification of personalities into two types—introverts and extroverts—became well known. He developed a theory of the unconscious mind, arguing that there were both personal, or individual, and inherited, or collective, elements.

From 1933 to 1941 Jung was professor of psychology at the Federal Polytechnical University in Zürich and from 1943 at the University of Basel. He also wrote many books. *Modern Man in Search of a Soul*, published in 1933, became a classic statement of the problems of 20th-century life. The semiautobiographical *Memories, Dreams, Reflections* was published after his death. He died in Küsnacht, Switzerland, on June 6, 1961.

# CHAPTER 29

# FLORENCE RENA SABIN

American anatomist Florence Rena Sabin conducted pioneering investigations of the lymphatic system. She was considered to be one of the leading women scientists of the United States.

Sabin was born on Nov. 9, 1871, in Central City, Colo. After graduating from the Johns Hopkins University Medical School in Baltimore, Md., in 1900, she interned at Johns Hopkins Hospital for a year and then returned to the medical school to conduct research under a fellowship awarded by the Baltimore Association for the Advancement of University Education of Women. In 1901 she published *An Atlas of the Medulla and Midbrain*, which became a popular medical text. In 1902, when Johns Hopkins finally abandoned its policy of not appointing women to its medical faculty, Sabin was named an assistant in anatomy, and she became in 1917 the school's first female full professor.

*Florence Rena Sabin.* Courtesy of the National Library of Medicine

For a number of years Sabin's research centered on the lymphatic system, and her demonstration that lymphatic vessels develop from a special layer of cells in certain fetal veins, rather than, as prevailing theory held, from intercellular spaces, established her as a researcher of the first rank. She then turned to the study of blood, blood vessels, and blood cells and made numerous discoveries regarding their origin and development. In 1924 she was elected president of the American Association of Anatomists, and in 1925 she was elected to the National Academy of Sciences; in both cases she was the first woman to be so honored.

Also in 1925 she accepted an invitation to join the Rockefeller Institute for Medical Research (now Rockefeller University), where she was also the first woman member. There she conducted research on tuberculosis. Sabin retired from the Rockefeller Institute in 1938 and moved to Denver, where in 1944 she was named by the governor to a planning committee on postwar public health problems. She drew up a plan and lobbied successfully for a complete reorganization of the state health department. In 1948 she was appointed head of the Denver health department. She died in Denver on Oct. 3, 1953.

# Chapter 30

# Alexander Fleming

Penicillin was discovered in September 1928. It has saved millions of lives by stopping the growth of the bacteria that are responsible for blood poisoning and many other once fatal diseases. This miracle drug was discovered and given to the world by Alexander Fleming, a physician and research bacteriologist at St. Mary's Hospital Medical School in London.

Alexander Fleming was born on Aug. 6, 1881, at Lochfield, Ayrshire, Scotland. He grew up on a farm. For two years he attended Kilmarnock Academy. When he was 13 years old he went to London to live with an older brother. He worked for five years as a clerk in a shipping company. When he was 20 he won a scholarship to St. Mary's Hospital Medical School. Fleming won practically every academic honor and on his graduation was offered a position as research bacteriologist with the hospital. He was associated with St. Mary's for the rest of his life. In the last years of his life he was director of its Wright-Fleming Institute of Microbiology.

In World War I Fleming served as a medical captain, specializing in the study and treatment of wounds. He was deeply impressed by the high death rate from bacterial infection of wounds. His discovery of penicillin greatly reduced the death rate from wounds in World War II.

Fleming was studying deadly bacteria in 1928 when he made his dramatic discovery. Always retiring and modest, he attributed it to "the greatest fortune." However, it was fortune combined with a gift for scientific observation and a genius for research.

For examination purposes Fleming had removed the cover of the bacteria culture plate with which he was working. A mold formed on the exposed culture. A less gifted scientist would have thrown away the accidentally contaminated culture. Fleming, however, noticed that in the area surrounding the mold, the bacteria had disappeared.

He kept a strain of the mold alive and began testing it on laboratory animals. In 1929 he published his first medical paper proving that a lowly mold from soil was a powerful microbe killer that did not injure human tissue.

*Sir Alexander Fleming in his laboratory at the Wright-Fleming Institute of Microbiology in London, c. 1955.* Peter Purdy/Hulton Archive/Getty Images

For years chemists were unable to extract enough pure concentrated penicillin to use in medicine. Fleming kept his mold, but the world of science almost forgot it. Then in 1938 a team of Oxford University scientists, headed by Howard Florey and Ernst B. Chain, remembered the research paper of nine years earlier. World War II interfered with the large-scale manufacture of penicillin in Great Britain. But methods for its mass production, purification, and stabilization were developed in the United States, in cooperation with the Department of Agriculture. Fleming was knighted in 1944 in recognition of his work. He also discovered lysozyme, an antibacterial agent in tears and saliva. In 1945 he shared the Nobel Prize for Physiology or Medicine with Florey and Chain. Fleming died in London on March 11, 1955.

# CHAPTER 31

# MARGARET SANGER

The founder of the birth-control movement in the United States was Margaret Sanger, a nurse who worked among the poor on the Lower East Side of New York City. There she witnessed firsthand the results of uncontrolled fertility, self-induced abortions, and high rates of infant and maternal mortality.

Sanger was born Margaret Higgins in Corning, N.Y., on Sept. 14, 1883. She took her nurse's training at the White Plains Hospital and the Manhattan Eye and Ear Clinic. She married William Sanger in 1900. Although she later divorced him she kept the last name by which she had become well known, even after she remarried in 1922.

Sanger believed in a woman's right to plan the size of her family. In 1912 she gave up nursing to devote herself full time to the cause of birth control. In 1914 she founded the National Birth Control League and in

*Margaret Sanger in her groundbreaking birth-control clinic in Brooklyn, NY.* Keystone-France/Gamma-Keystone/Getty Images

that same year was indicted for sending out copies of the periodical *The Woman Rebel,* which advocated birth control. At that time the federal Comstock Law of 1873 classified such literature as obscene. Her case was dismissed in 1916. Later that year she opened the first birth-control clinic in the United States in Brooklyn, N.Y. She was arrested and served 20 days in jail in 1917 for creating a public nuisance. Continued government harassment brought public opinion to her side, and in 1936 the 1873 law was modified.

In 1921 Sanger founded the American Birth Control League and served as its president until 1928. That and later organizations became in 1942 the Planned Parenthood Federation of America. Sanger organized the first World Population Conference in Geneva, Switzerland, in 1927 and was also the first president of the International Planned Parenthood Federation, organized in 1953. She helped promote family planning in India and Japan. She wrote several books, including *My Fight for Birth Control* (1931). Sanger died in Tucson, Ariz., on Sept. 6, 1966.

# CHAPTER 32

# FREDERICK GRANT BANTING

Diabetes, once a fatal disease, can now be controlled with insulin, a substance discovered by the Canadian surgeon Frederick Grant Banting and his assistant, Charles Herbert Best.

Frederick Grant Banting was born on a farm near Alliston, Ont., on Nov. 14, 1891. He studied medicine at the University of Toronto and received his M.D. in 1916. After serving in World War I, he began practice as a surgeon in London, Ont. He also taught physiology at the University of Western Ontario.

One evening in October 1920 Banting was preparing a class lecture on the pancreas. It was known that diabetes was caused by a disturbance of the pancreas that kept the body from making use of sugar. It appeared that the substance involved was a hormone secreted directly into the bloodstream from small cell clusters called the

*Charles Herbert Best and Frederick Grant Banting with one of the first diabetic dogs to receive insulin treatments, c. 1921.* Hulton Archive/Getty Images

islands of Langerhans, but the pancreas also secretes digestive juices. Attempts to isolate the hormone had always failed. The reason seemed to be that when a pancreas was removed from an animal the digestive juices destroyed the hormone.

Banting read that if the pancreatic duct was tied off, the digestive-juice cells shriveled and died. He wrote: "Tie off the pancreatic duct of dogs. Wait six to eight weeks for degeneration. Remove residue and extract." The next summer Banting went to the University of Toronto and asked Professor J.J.R. MacLeod for a laboratory and dogs. MacLeod agreed and had Charles Best appointed as Banting's assistant. Best was still a medical student, but he was an expert on blood-sugar measurement.

The two worked for weeks. On July 30, 1921, they removed the pancreas from one of the dogs whose pancreatic duct had been tied off. They ground up the gland and prepared a solution. The dog had sunk into a diabetic coma, they injected the solution into its veins, and within a few hours the dog was walking again. By 1923 the drug was available in quantity from the pancreatic glands of slaughtered cattle. It was named insulin from the Latin for *island* (after the islets, or islands, of Langerhans).

The Nobel Prize for Medicine was divided in 1923 between Banting and MacLeod. Banting felt that Best had been slighted and gave him half his own share. In 1930 the University of Toronto honored him with the dedication of the Banting Institute. There he continued his medical research and, in 1934, he was knighted. Banting was killed in an airplane crash in Newfoundland on Feb. 21, 1941.

CHAPTER 33

# BARBARA McCLINTOCK

In the 1940s and 1950s American geneticist Barbara McClintock discovered that chromosomes can break off from neighboring chromosomes and recombine to create unique genetic combinations in a process known as crossing over, a radical break from accepted genetic doctrine of the time. The importance of her research, performed on corn (maize), was not recognized for many years. Only after geneticists found other movable genetic elements, such as transposons, in both plants and animals was McClintock acknowledged for her role in explaining complicated patterns of inheritance. She was awarded the 1983 Nobel Prize for Physiology or Medicine, the first woman ever to win an unshared prize in that category.

Barbara McClintock was born on June 16, 1902, in Hartford, Conn., and was reared in New York City. She earned her doctorate in botany at Cornell University in 1927 and remained there until 1941 to do research work with the "Cornell corn group" of R.A. Emerson, George Beadle, Marcus Rhoades, and Charles Burnham. At the end of 1941 she began her long association with the Cold Spring Harbor Laboratory in Long Island, N.Y., where she worked in almost total isolation for 50 years.

Despite her maverick reputation she garnered many honors, including the National Medal of Science in 1970, and she became president of the Genetics Society in 1945. At the time of her death on Sept. 2, 1992, in Huntington, N.Y., many of her colleagues agreed that she was one of the most important figures in the history of genetics.

# CHAPTER 34

# CHARLES RICHARD DREW

African American physician and surgeon Charles Richard Drew was an authority on the preservation of human blood for transfusion.

Drew was born on June 3, 1904, in Washington, D.C. He was educated at Amherst College (graduated 1926), McGill University, Montreal (1933), and Columbia University (1940). While earning his doctorate at Columbia in the late 1930s, he conducted research into the properties and preservation of blood plasma. He soon developed efficient ways to process and store large quantities of blood plasma in "blood banks." As the leading authority in the field, he organized and directed the blood-plasma programs of the United States and Great Britain in the early years of World War II, while also agitating the authorities to stop excluding the blood of African Americans from plasma-supply networks.

*Charles Richard Drew in 1946.* Alfred Eisenstaedt/Time & Life Pictures/ Getty Images

Drew resigned his official posts in 1942 after the armed forces ruled that the blood of African Americans would be accepted but would have to be stored separately from that of whites. He then became a surgeon and professor of medicine at Freedmen's Hospital, Washington, D.C., and Howard University (1942–50). He was fatally injured in an automobile accident on April 1, 1950, near Burlington, N.C.

# Chapter 35

# Albert Sabin

Polish-born U.S. physician and microbiologist Albert Sabin was a towering figure in medical research who in 1955 developed the first oral vaccine for poliomyelitis (polio), which was administered to millions of children in Europe, Africa, and the Americas beginning in the late 1950s. His live, weakened vaccine, which was dispensed on a sugar cube or in liquid, was easier to administer and provided longer protection than the killed, injected vaccine developed by Jonas Salk. Both vaccines, however, were credited with virtually eradicating the crippling and sometimes fatal effects of polio, a scourge that, at its peak in 1952, paralyzed 21,000 Americans and killed 3,100.

Sabin was born in Bialystok, Poland, on Aug. 26, 1906. He immigrated to the United States in 1921 with his family, and two cousins taught him enough English to make it possible for him to enter high school. Ten years later he earned an M.D. degree from New York University. He served two years as house physician at Bellevue Hospital in New York City before attending the Lister Institute of Preventive Medicine in London. After returning to New York City in 1935, he joined the staff of the Rockefeller Institute for Medical Research, where he was the first to demonstrate the growth of poliovirus in human nervous tissue outside the body. In 1939, after becoming associate professor of pediatrics at the University of Cincinnati College of Medicine in Ohio, he served as chief of the college's division of infectious diseases at the Children's Hospital Research Foundation (1939-43). During World War II he interrupted his polio research to work with the U.S. Army Medical Corps. Sabin isolated the virus that caused sandfly fever, which was epidemic among U.S. troops in Africa, and he later developed vaccines against dengue fever and Japanese encephalitis.

After the war he returned to the University of Cincinnati and served as professor of research pediatrics (1946-60) and distinguished service professor (1960-71) before becoming professor emeritus in 1971. Though he was paralyzed in 1983 with polyneuritis, an inflammation of the nerve cells, he made almost a full recovery and continued working on a measles vaccine before retiring in 1988. Sabin was elected to the National Academy of Sciences in 1951 and was the recipient of the U.S. Medals of Science (1970), Freedom (1986), and Liberty (1986). He died on March 3, 1993, in Washington, D.C.

# Chapter 36

# Jonas Salk

For the first half of the 20th century, polio was one of the most dreaded diseases to attack young people. By 1955 American physician and researcher Jonas Salk had developed a vaccine that almost eradicated the disease in the United States and other developed countries.

Jonas Edward Salk was born in New York City on Oct. 28, 1914. He graduated from the City College of New York in 1934 and earned his doctorate in medicine from New York University's College of Medicine in 1939. While in medical school he had worked with Thomas Francis, Jr., on killed-virus immunology studies. In 1942 he joined a group at the University of Michigan working on a vaccine against influenza. The vaccine was perfected in 1953.

In 1947 Salk became associate professor of bacteriology and head of the Virus Research Laboratory at the University of Pittsburgh School of Medicine. There he began working on the polio vaccine. Three

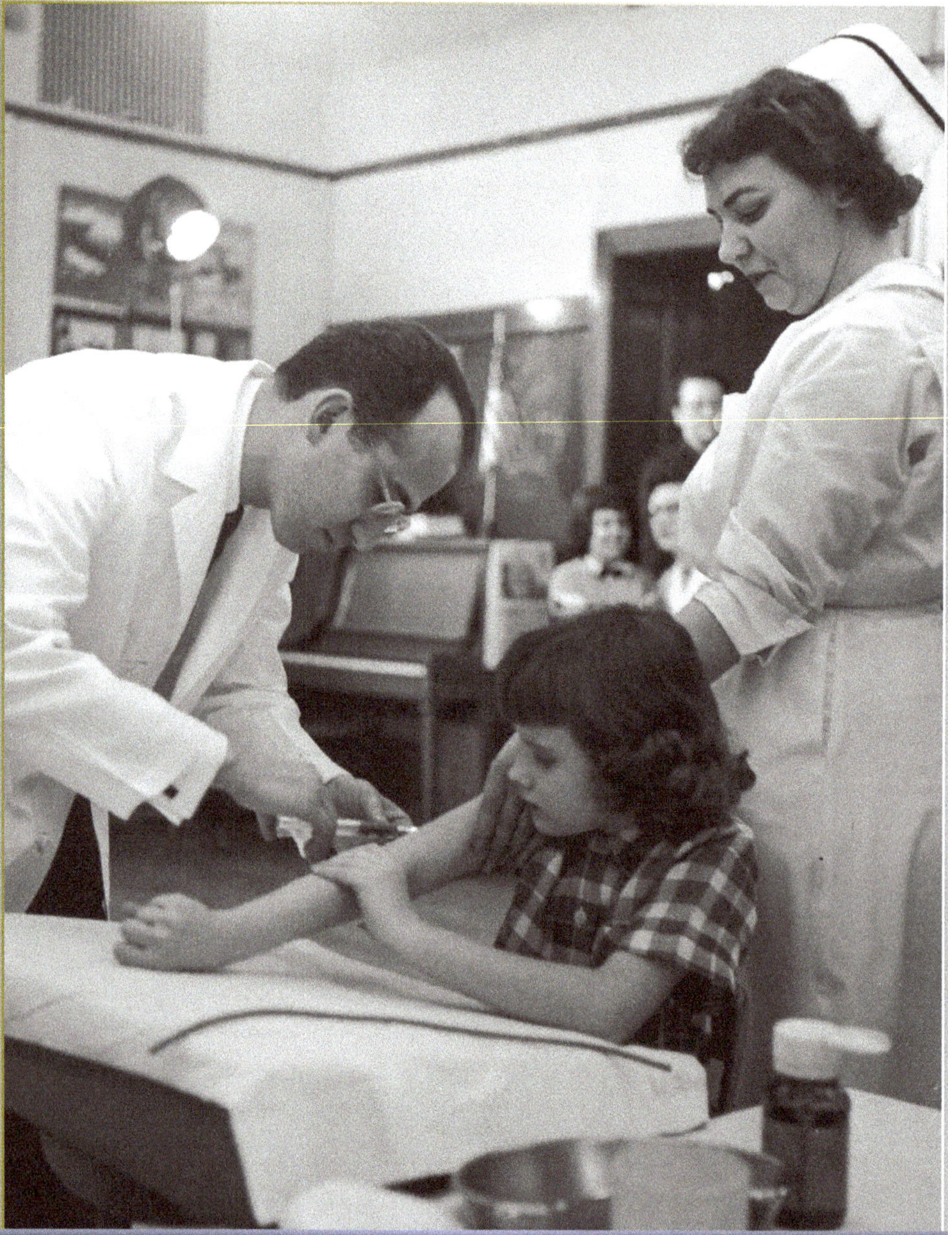

*Jonas Salk, aided by a nurse, vaccinating a girl against polio in 1953.* Archive Photos/Getty Images

viruses caused polio, and a vaccine had to be effective against all of them. By 1952 Salk had developed such a vaccine and conducted field tests on children. His findings were published in 1953, and a mass field test was done the next year.

On April 12, 1955, the vaccine was released for use in the United States. In 1957 Salk was named professor of experimental medicine at Pittsburgh, and in 1963 he went to San Diego as head of the Institute (later named the Salk Institute) for Biological Studies. In 1977 Salk was awarded the Presidential Medal of Freedom. He died on June 23, 1995, in La Jolla, Calif.

# CHAPTER 37

# FRANCIS CRICK

British biochemist Francis Crick helped make one of the most important discoveries of 20th-century biology—the determination of the molecular structure of deoxyribonucleic acid (DNA). For this accomplishment, Crick received, with colleagues James D. Watson and Maurice Wilkins, the 1962 Nobel Prize for Physiology or Medicine.

Francis Harry Compton Crick was born on June 8, 1916, in Northampton, Northamptonshire, England. He was educated at University College, London. During World War II, he helped develop magnetic mines for naval use, and from 1949 to 1977 he was on the staff of Cambridge University's Cavendish Laboratories.

In 1951, when Watson arrived at Cambridge, it was known that the mysterious nucleic acids, especially DNA, played a central role in the hereditary determination of the structure and function of each cell. Watson convinced Crick that knowledge

*Francis Crick in 1993.* Daniel Mordzinski/AFP/Getty Images

of DNA's three-dimensional structure would make its hereditary role apparent. Using X-ray diffraction studies of DNA done by Wilkins (X-ray diffraction being a technique that allows scientists to investigate the structure of different materials), Watson and Crick were able to construct a molecular model consistent with the known physical and chemical properties of DNA. The model consisted of two intertwined helical (spiral) strands of sugar-phosphate, bridged horizontally by flat organic bases.

Crick later discovered that each group of three bases (a codon) on a single DNA strand designates the position of a specific amino acid on the backbone of a protein molecule. He also helped determine which codons code for each amino acid normally found in protein, thus clarifying the way the cell uses DNA to build proteins.

Crick was elected to the U.S. National Academy of Sciences in 1969. From 1977 he held the position of distinguished professor at the Salk Institute for Biological Studies in San Diego, Calif. He published a number of books, including *Of Molecules and Men* (1966), *What Mad Pursuit: A Personal View of Scientific Discovery* (1988), and *The Astonishing Hypothesis* (1994). He was awarded the Order of Merit in 1991. Crick died on July 28, 2004, in San Diego.

# CHAPTER 38

# CHRISTIAAN BARNARD

In 1967, South African surgeon Christiaan Barnard made medical history. As the head of the surgical team that performed the first successful human heart transplant, Barnard forever changed the approach taken toward the procedure and profoundly altered the course of modern cardiac surgery.

Christiaan Neethling Barnard was born on Nov. 8, 1922, in Beaufort West, South Africa. His father was an Afrikaner preacher, and his mother was a homemaker. As a young adult, Barnard studied medicine at the University of Cape Town in South Africa. After receiving his degree, he first went into general practice on the Western Cape, and then established himself as a general surgeon at the Groote Schuur Hospital in Cape Town. He became increasingly interested in cardiology, however, and in the late 1950s engaged in postgraduate studies in cardiac surgery at the University of Minnesota in the United States.

When he returned to South Africa in 1958, Barnard established himself as a cardiothoracic (heart and chest) surgeon at Groote Schuur. Among other milestones, he performed open-heart surgery in South Africa and developed new designs for replacement heart valves. Determined to find a viable technique for heart transplant, he performed many experimental surgeries on animals in his labs. In late 1967 Louis Washkansky, a South African grocer with end-stage heart disease, agreed to allow Barnard to perform a heart transplant on him. Using a heart taken from a fatally injured accident victim, Barnard led a 20-member team in the transplant procedure on Dec. 3, 1967. Although the surgery itself was successful, Washkansky died less than three weeks later of complications from pneumonia.

Barnard continued to develop his transplant technique over the following years. By the late 1970s, his approach had improved to the point that many of his patients survived for several years following surgery. In

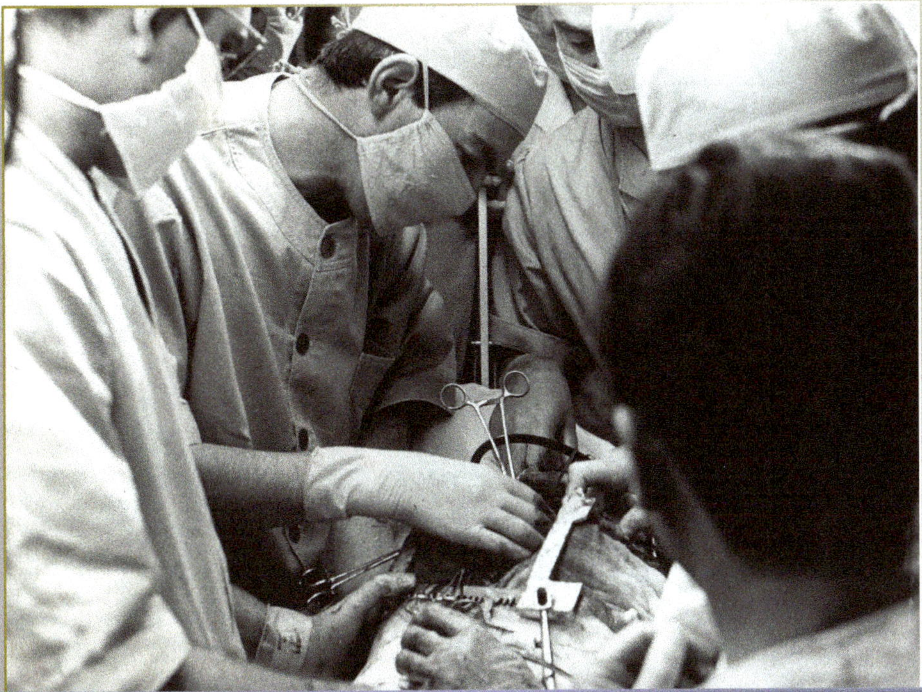

*Pioneering heart surgeon Christiaan Barnard performing an operation, c. 1970.* Paul Popper/Popperfoto/Getty Images

1983, Barnard retired from surgical practice. He authored several books, including *Christiaan Barnard: One Life* (1969), *The Second Life* (1993), and *50 Ways to a Healthy Heart* (2001). He died on Sept. 2, 2001, in Paphos, Cyprus, following an acute asthma attack.

Chapter 39

# Elisabeth Kübler-Ross

Swiss-born American psychiatrist and author Elisabeth Kübler-Ross was a pioneer in the study of death and dying whose work helped revolutionize the care of the terminally ill and helped change attitudes toward pain control and death itself. She was especially known for having identified five stages of grief experienced by the dying: denial, anger, bargaining, depression, and acceptance.

Kübler-Ross was born on July 8, 1926, in Zürich, Switzerland. She knew at a young age that she wanted to be a doctor and defied her father's plans for her to be his secretary in the business he managed. Instead, she worked at a variety of jobs and, when World War II ended, did volunteer relief work in Poland before studying at the University of Zürich, from which she received her medical degree in 1957. She moved to the United States the following year and was disturbed to discover the medical community's tendency to refuse to acknowledge the reality of death to terminally ill patients and therefore to deny those patients the help they needed for dealing with it. In the early 1960s, as a teaching fellow at the University of Colorado's medical school, Kübler-Ross began to try to enlighten her students on the subject, and while working in Chicago, she held seminars in which the terminally ill were interviewed and allowed to express themselves.

It was from these interviews that she developed her description of the five stages, which she set forth in her best-selling *On Death and Dying* (1969). Gradually, the medical profession adopted new methods of treating patients at the end of life. In the 1970s, however, Kübler-Ross became enamored of more eccentric views—out-of-body experiences, spirit guides, and psychic channeling, for example—that diminished her reputation in the eyes of many people.

Kübler-Ross wrote more than 20 books, including her autobiography, *The Wheel of Life: A Memoir of Living and Dying* (1997) and *On Grief and Grieving* (2005). She died on Aug. 24, 2004, in Scottsdale, Ariz.

# CHAPTER 40

# OLIVER SACKS

British neurologist and writer Oliver Sacks won acclaim for his sympathetic case histories of patients with unusual neurological disorders.

Sacks was born on July 9, 1933, in London. He attended Queen's College, Oxford, where he received a bachelor's degree in physiology in 1954 and a medical degree in 1958. He completed an internship at Middlesex Hospital in London in 1959 and served as house surgeon of Queen Elizabeth Hospital in Birmingham in 1960. Sacks left England for the United States to accept an internship at Mt. Zion Hospital in San Francisco (1961–62) before serving as a resident in neurology (1962–65) at the University of California, Los Angeles.

In 1965 Sacks became an instructor at Albert Einstein College of Medicine in the Bronx borough of New York City, where he remained, eventually becoming a clinical professor of neurology (1966–75). He also joined Beth Abraham Hospital, a charity

*Oliver Sacks outside his childhood home, c. 1986.* Sahm Doherty/Time & Life Pictures/Getty Images

institution in the Bronx, as a staff neurologist (1966–2007). There he met a group of patients who had contracted a sleeping sickness, encephalitis lethargica, during an epidemic that broke out between 1917 and 1927. The patients had survived only to develop a type of parkinsonism that caused varying degrees of immobility, speechlessness, and depression. Sacks recounted the brief cure that the patients experienced after receiving the drug l-dopa and the drug's subsequent side effects in his 1973 book *Awakenings*, which was made into a motion picture in 1990.

Sacks enumerated further experiences, both professional and personal, to a wide audience. Having injured a leg in a mountaineering accident, he learned firsthand how a physician's dismissal of a patient's condition could hinder recuperation, a saga he related in *A Leg to Stand On* (1984). In *Seeing Voices* (1989), he explored the ways in which sign language not only provides the deaf with a means of communication but also serves as the foundation for a discrete culture. In *An Anthropologist on Mars* (1995), he documented the lives of seven patients living with conditions ranging from autism to brain damage and described the unique ways in which they created functional lives in spite of their disabilities.

Sacks described his journey to Micronesia to study a population with a high incidence of color blindness and to Guam to study a mysterious form of paralysis in *The Island of the Colorblind* (1997). He wrote of patients with conditions relating to music in *Musicophilia: Tales of Music and the Brain* (2007). Included among his autobiographical works are *Uncle Tungsten: Memories of a Chemical Boyhood* (2001) and *Oaxaca Journal* (2002).

In 1989 Sacks received a Guggenheim Fellowship for his studies of the influence of culture on the aberrant (abnormal) neurological processes underlying the rare inherited disease known as Tourette syndrome. In addition to his position at Beth Abraham, he served as professor of neurology at the New York University School of Medicine (1992–2007) and the New York University Comprehensive Epilepsy Center (1999–2007). In 2007 Sacks became a professor of neurology and psychiatry at the Columbia University Medical Center in New York. Sacks was made Commander of the British Empire in 2008. Though he resided permanently in the United States, he never relinquished British citizenship.

# Chapter 41

# Francis Collins

American geneticist Francis Collins discovered genes causing genetic diseases and led the U.S. National Institutes of Health (NIH) public research consortium in the Human Genome Project (HGP). In 2009 Pres. Barack Obama nominated Collins to head the NIH, a move that was confirmed by the U.S. Senate in August of that year.

Collins was born on April 14, 1950, in Staunton, Va. He received a B.S. from the University of Virginia (1970), went on to Yale University to earn an M.S. and a Ph.D. (1974), and earned an M.D. (1977) at the University of North Carolina at Chapel Hill. In 1984 Collins joined the staff of the University of Michigan at Ann Arbor as an assistant professor. His work at Michigan would earn him a reputation as one of the world's foremost genetics researchers. In 1989 he announced the discovery of the gene that causes cystic fibrosis. The following year a Collins-led team found the gene that causes neurofibromatosis, a genetic disorder that generates the growth of tumors. He also served as a leading researcher in a collaboration of six laboratories that in 1993 uncovered the gene that causes Huntington chorea, a neurological disease.

In 1993 Collins, by then a full professor, left Michigan to take the post as head of the National Human Genome Research Institute (NHGRI) of the NIH, which had begun work on the HGP three years earlier with a stated goal of completing the sequencing project in 15 years at a cost of $3 billion. The necessity of a government effort was questioned, however, when a rival operation, Celera Genomics, emerged in 1998 and appeared to be working even faster than the HGP at deciphering the human deoxyribonucleic acid (DNA) sequence. Headed by American geneticist and businessman J. Craig Venter, a former NIH scientist, Celera had devised its own, quicker method—though some scientists, Collins among them, questioned the accuracy of the work.

In the end the public and private endeavors came together. On June 26, 2000, Collins, Venter, and U.S. Pres. Bill Clinton

*Francis Collins.* National Institutes of Health

gathered in Washington, D.C., to announce that the rough draft sequence of the DNA in the human genetic map had been completed through the combined effort of Collins's public research consortium and Venter's private company. The breakthrough was hailed as the first step toward helping doctors diagnose, treat, and even prevent thousands of illnesses caused by genetic disorders. In April 2003, following further analysis of the sequence, the HGP came to a close. The announcement of the completion of the HGP coincided with the 50th anniversary of American geneticist and biophysicist James D. Watson and British biophysicist Francis Crick's publication on the structure of DNA.

A practicing Christian, Collins freely expressed the awe he experienced as a leader in the uncloaking of one of the mysteries of life. As concerns arose about the moral and ethical implications of the research he had conducted, Collins actively cautioned against misuse of genetic information. At congressional hearings in July 2000, Collins urged the passage of federal law to set guidelines on how individuals' genetic information could be handled.

"The potential for mischief is quite great," he said. On Aug. 1, 2008, Collins resigned from his position as director of the NHGRI in order to pursue broader, more flexible research opportunities. In October 2009, following his Senate confirmation to head the NIH, Collins was appointed by Pope Benedict XVI to the Pontifical Academy of Sciences, an organization that promotes advancement in the fundamental understanding of scientific questions and the investigation of ethical and philosophical issues associated with science.

# Chapter 42

# Margaret Chan

Chinese civil servant Margaret Chan has served as director general of the World Health Organization (WHO) since 2007.

Chan was born in Hong Kong in 1947. She attended Northcote College of Education in Hong Kong before moving to Canada, where she earned B.A. (1973) and M.D. (1977) degrees from the University of Western Ontario. She also received a Master of Science degree in public health (1985) from Singapore National University. She joined the Hong Kong Department of Health in 1978 and became its director in 1994. She served as director for nine years, during which time she focused on communicable disease surveillance and response and on improving training for public health professionals.

Chan's leadership during a time of crisis was widely commended after the first human cases of the deadly H5N1 bird flu virus appeared in Hong Kong in 1997. Her response included an order to destroy the city's entire poultry stock—some 1.5 million birds. The order, carried out within three days, allowed authorities to bring the outbreak under control and possibly avert a pandemic. Chan also elevated her international profile with her management of the 2003 SARS outbreak, which claimed the lives of nearly 300 persons in Hong Kong, though some critics faulted her for not acting more aggressively after the outbreak initially appeared in China's neighboring Guangdong province.

From 2003 to 2005 Chan served as director of WHO's Department of Protection of the Human Environment, and from 2005 until 2007 she was WHO's assistant director general for communicable diseases. Chan succeeded Lee Jong Wook of South Korea as director general of WHO a few months after his unexpected death. She and 10 other candidates were recommended for the post by their respective governments, and, after four rounds of balloting by WHO's executive board, Chan emerged as the nominee. Her selection was confirmed during a special session of the World Health Assembly on November 9. Supporters praised Chan's ability in handling crisis situations, pointing

*World Health Organization director general Margaret Chan on May 17, 2010, at the UN offices in Geneva, Switzerland, addressing the WHO regarding the swine flu pandemic.* Fabrice Coffrini/AFP/Getty Images

to her experience in managing the bird flu and SARS outbreaks.

Chan officially became director general in early January 2007. In her first speech after taking the position, she outlined her specific goals of improving the health of people in Africa and of women around the world. "All regions, all countries, all people are equally important," she stated, "but we must focus our attention on the people in greatest need."

In 2009, during an ongoing outbreak of swine flu that began in Mexico and subsequently spread to countries worldwide, Chan was confronted with the difficult task of assessing the potential global health impact of the disease. On June 11, 2009, following a series of meetings with an emergency committee from whom she sought scientific evidence on which to base her decision, Chan officially declared the swine flu outbreak a pandemic. It was the first pandemic to be declared since the Hong Kong flu pandemic of 1968. The worldwide death toll from the swine flu virus was estimated by the WHO at 18,500 at the time that Chan announced the official end of the pandemic on Aug.

10, 2010. Later that year, Chan cowrote an article in which she maintained that the "opportunity to end all deaths from malaria by 2015 is within our reach" and urged international cooperation toward that goal.

# CONCLUSION

Since ancient times, healers with varying degrees of knowledge and skills have sought to restore the health or relieve the distress of the sick and injured. Often, that meant doing little more than offering sympathy to the patient while nature took its course. Today, however, practitioners of medicine have several millennia of medical advances on which to base the care of their patients.

This volume has detailed many of those advances along with the lives and careers of the pioneering men and women who helped to bring them about. While ancient practitioners did not entirely lack valid medical knowledge, much of early medicine was closely identified with pagan religions and superstition. It was Hippocrates who showed that disease had natural—rather than supernatural—causes. Following Hippocratic concepts, Galen later conducted many scientific experiments and produced writings that proved important to the beginnings of modern science during the Renaissance.

During the 17th and 18th centuries, impressive scientific progress was made in the fields of anatomy, chemistry, and microbiology, as reflected in the achievements of William Harvey, Marcello Malpighi, Anthony van Leeuwenhoek, Edward Jenner, and others. Certainly one of the most important advances of the 19th century was the development and acceptance of the germ theory of disease, for which Louis Pasteur and Robert Koch are given much of the credit. The germ theory's acceptance led to improved health practices, methods of food production, sanitation, and antiseptic surgical methods.

One of the greatest accomplishments of the 20th century was the success in treating infectious diseases. A public health vaccination program eradicated smallpox globally by 1979, and the landmark work of researchers such as Jonas Salk and Albert Sabin enabled the elimination of polio in most parts of the world by the beginning of the 21st century.

In recent decades, significant progress has also been made in another area of medical inquiry—understanding how genetic information is passed along. In particular, the Human Genome Project, completed in 2003, represented one of the boldest scientific undertakings in history and yielded genetic information that has allowed researchers to pinpoint errors in genes that cause or contribute to disease. Advances continue to be made toward realizing the goal of truly personalized medicine—individualized treatment that will be based on the knowledge of a patient's entire genome sequence.

# GLOSSARY

**autism** A disorder of early development that causes severe problems in thinking, communicating with others, and feeling a part of the outside world.

**blood platelet** One of the minute disks of the blood of a vertebrate animal that assist in blood clotting.

**corpuscle** One of the very small cells (as a red blood cell) that float freely in the blood.

**cowpox** A mild disease of the cow that when passed on to human beings produces a temporary rash and protects against smallpox.

**fermentation** Chemical breaking down of an organic substance (as in the souring of milk) produced by an enzyme and often accompanied by the formation of a gas.

**genome** The genetic material of an organism. There are about 25,000–30,000 genes in the human genome.

**histology** A branch of anatomy that deals with the study of animal and plant tissues.

**insulin** A hormone that is produced by the pancreas and is necessary for the normal use of sugar by the body.

**libido** Sexual drive or instinct.

**lymphatic system** A system in humans and many animals consisting of tissues and organs that work to protect the body from damage by foreign materials.

**lysozyme** A bacteria-destroying enzyme found in egg whites, tears, and saliva.

**pandemic** More widespread than an epidemic, a pandemic is the outbreak of a disease over a wide geographic area affecting an exceptionally high proportion of the population.

**parasite** An organism that lives on or inside another organism, a parasite depends on the other organism (called a host) for food.

**Parkinsonism** A chronic progressive disorder of the nervous system seen in middle or late life that is marked by muscle tremors and weakness, slowness of movement, impaired balance, and a shuffling gait. It is also known as Parkinson's disease.

**pestilence** A contagious or infectious epidemic disease that spreads quickly and is often fatal.

**physiology** The study of the function of life and living things (such as organs, tissues, and cells) and how they work together.

**poliomyelitis (polio)** An infectious viral disease marked by inflammation of nerve cells in the spinal cord accompanied by fever and often paralysis and wasting of muscles.

**protozoan** Generally microscopic, single-celled organism with a distinct nucleus that is unable to make its own food and eats other organisms. For this reason, protozoans were once considered animals.

**septum** A dividing wall or membrane, especially between bodily spaces or masses of soft tissue.

**syphilis** A venereal disease that is caused by a spirochete, is usually sexually transmitted, and if left untreated is marked by a series of three stages extending over many years.

American Institute of Biological Sciences (AIBS)
1900 Campus Commons Drive
Suite 200
Reston, VA 20191
(703) 674-2500
Web site: http://www.aibs.org
Committed to advancing research and education in all aspects of the biological sciences, AIBS creates a number of programs and resources for students and the public at large, such as its ActionBioscience.org Web site. AIBS also advocates for a number of policy initiatives directed at the biological sciences community.

Canadian Institutes of Health Research (CIHR)
160 Elgin Street, 9th Floor
Address Locator: 4809A
Ottawa, ON K1S 0W9
Canada
(613) 941-2672
Web site: http://www.cihr-irsc.gc.ca
Comprised of 13 “virtual” institutes, the

CIHR funds health research on a wide variety of health concerns. Its integrated and interdisciplinary research has helped advance understanding of such health concerns as aging, cancer, and addiction.

Canadian Medical Association (CMA)
1867 Alta Vista Drive
Ottawa, ON K1G 5W8
Canada
(888) 855-2555
Web site: http://www.cma.ca
The CMA provides clinical and networking resources to students and physicians dedicated to promoting excellence in Canada's health services.

J. Craig Venter Institute (JCVI)
9704 Medical Center Drive
Rockville, MD 20850
(301) 795-7000
Web site: http://www.jcvi.org
The JCVI takes a multidisciplinary approach to genomics-centered research and has been at the forefront of scientific discovery. Its DiscoverGenomics! Science Education Program offers opportunities for development for both

students and educators interested in bringing genomics to the classroom.

National Institutes of Health (NIH)
9000 Rockville Pike
Bethesda, Maryland 20892
(301) 496-4000
Web site: http://www.nih.gov
With twenty-seven institutes and centers dedicated to medical and public health research, the NIH advances understanding of key health issues affecting the population including cancer, heart disease, and diabetes, among a wide range of others.

World Health Organization (WHO)
Avenue Appia 20
1211 Geneva 27
Switzerland
+ 41 22 791 21 11
Web site: http://www.who.int
The WHO coordinates global health initiatives for the United Nations and provides important research and leadership necessary for addressing health concerns around the world.

## Web Sites

Due to the changing nature of Internet links, Rosen Educational Services has developed an online list of Web sites related to the subject of this book. This site is updated regularly. Please use this link to access the list:

http://www.rosenlinks.com/inven/medpi

http://www.uab.edu/reynolds/exhibits/histfigs

http://www.nlm.nih.gov/changingthefaceofmedicine/

http://profiles.nlm.nih.gov/

http://clendening.kumc.edu/dc/fn/

http://www.nyu.edu/projects/sanger/

http://www.pbs.org/wgbh/aso/databank/medhealth.html

http://www.imperial.nhs.uk/aboutus/museumsandarchives/

# BIBLIOGRAPHY


Adler, Robert. *Medical Firsts: From Hippocrates to the Human Genome* (John Wiley & Sons, 2004).

Bynum, W.F. *History of Medicine: A Very Short Introduction* (Oxford University Press, 2008).

Groopman, Jerome. *How Doctors Think* (Houghton Mifflin, 2007).

Harding, Anne S. *Milestones in Health and Medicine* (Oryx Press, 2000).

Jauhar, Sandeep. *Intern: A Doctor's Initiation* (Farrar, Straus and Giroux, 2008

Nuland, Sherwin B. *The Uncertain Art: Thoughts on a Life in Medicine* (Random House, 2008).

Porter, Roy, ed. *Cambridge Illustrated History of Medicine* (Cambridge University Press, 2001).

Rutkow, Ira M. *Seeking the Cure: A History of Medicine in America* (Scribner, 2010).

Straus, Eugene W., and Straus, Alex. *Medical Marvels: The 100 Greatest Advances in Medicine* (Prometheus Books, 2006).

Yount, Lisa. *The History of Medicine* (Lucent, 2002).

# INDEX

## I



## J



## K



## L



## M

## N



## O



## P



## R